THE WILD ANGEL

E. C. SPYKMAN

The Wild Angel

HARCOURT, BRACE AND COMPANY, NEW YORK

LIBRARY OF CONGRESS CATALOG CARD NUMBER: 57-6778

PRINTED IN THE UNITED STATES OF AMERICA

To the two Josies

Contents

1. THEODORE'S CRUSADE   11

2. HUBERT'S LAMB   40

3. GRANDFATHER'S CITY HOUSE   67

4. FATHER'S FRIEND   93

5. THE HORTICULTURAL BALL   121

6. IT   149

7. POOR WIDGY   179

8. THE MARVELOUS KID   196

THE WILD ANGEL

CHAPTER ONE

Theodore's Crusade

Theodore Cares on a very early September morning in the year 1908, at the age of fourteen, and not long before he was going to have to go off to boarding school, was standing in the geranium bed of the Red House in Summerton, Massachusetts, where he lived, delicately holding the end of a string, the other end of which he thought might still be attached to his sister Edith's toe. He could not make up his mind whether to pull the string or not. His sister Edith was six, much too young to go on the expedition he was contemplating this morning, but, unfortunately, although she looked innocent in a pink and yellow way, Theodore had to admit that Edith was a blackmailer. How she had guessed he was going out early and what his errand was, he could not fathom. Probably Pat, the coachman, had been telling that terrible woman in the kitchen who was Cook what they had been saying at the blacksmith shop yesterday, and she had told Gander, the parlormaid, and Gander told Nurse. Nurse told Edie bits of things, and Edie did the rest by herself. She was very good at it.

Theodore squinted up at the window, making himself

as blind as possible so that he would not see any face looking out, and all at once he had to sit down. He had been
suddenly made to feel weak at the thought of all the females among whom he had to live. Gosh, Edie was *nothing*. Besides her there was Madam, Father's new wife,
whom he had married a year ago. Edie had killed their
real mother, as everyone knew, by having to get herself
born. Theodore picked up a dry stick and dug around a
geranium plant. Well, Madam had turned out all right. He
was not going to say more than that about any female,
but Madam was really all right. She was good-looking, she
could be fashionable by putting on a gigantic hat, and you
could depend on her to muzzle Father when he barked too
loud and too long, but she was a female just the same.
There were all those biddies in the kitchen. And there was
his dear sister Jane. Theodore threw the stick away violently. With the most precise precautions he had got out
his window and slid down the roof in order to fool Father's beagle, who slept in the hall. And Edie, he saw
clearly now, no matter what she had promised, would
wake up the house. That would mean Jane as well. He
would be darned if he would take two females with him.
Besides, Jane was the last straw. Somehow she had gotten
the idea into her head that girls were as good as boys.
Nothing would get it out. Heaven knows, he had tried. If
he showed Jane how feeble girls really were, she bit. If he
called her a hag just to get her to look a bit better, she said
that she looked just like him. She was eleven, thin, and
sandy, and freckled. It might be the same sort of face, but,

frankly, on a girl he did not think much of it. He kicked a hole with his heel in the soft dirt and thought for a moment of the only other male in the house except Father. This was Hubert, who was nine. He had no objection to Hubert. Although he looked somewhat like Edie, he was a good enough guy for a brother most of the time and not at all interested in right or wrong, but he had a terrible weakness. He could not see the sense in fighting.

"Your honor, you ass," Theodore had often told him. "You fight for your honor."

"I haven't got any," said Hubert frankly.

And what was worse, Hubert thought this a good thing. "If I had, with you and Jane around, I'd a been dead long ago."

Hubert was useless unless he got a kind of convulsion to make him tear headfirst into action. But he had to get a good punch on the nose to produce it. This was not the kind of person Theodore needed this morning. A cool head and generalship, his own qualities, were what must be used. He remembered the string and threw it up to the gutter so that nothing could come along and jerk Edie's toe off. Then he stepped out on the lawn.

Theodore stood and stretched. Jane might have said that he looked like a heron, but he felt like an eagle, and like an eagle he was going to be free. Everything around him— lawns, shrubs, walls, fences, gates, trees, and long wide meadows with their grass and cows, he felt—belonged to him. At any rate to his family. Aunts and uncles were spread around on the acres of their dairy farms as far as he could see anywhere, and Grandfather had his property next door. Aunt Charlotte was behind. The only exception was the McHenrys' right across the road. How did they get there? And there were also the Reservoir basins that ran in a chain like a quiet river right through town, the family lawns and pastures along their borders. They belonged to the Water Company. Well, never mind that. He, Theodore Cares, in Summerton, was a Prince of the Blood, and he liked it. At this very moment he liked so much the mist that was rising like a long thread from the open water and the great field of corn that he could see under the maples that bordered the Galway Road that he felt almost as if he were bursting. He had better get going to work it off. He meant to look after Summerton, the way the family had, for the rest of his life, and this morning he had to see about something that he had heard was going on at the farthest end of his kingdom. Yesterday he had had to get his polo pony, Cinder, shod at the blacksmith shop, and he had heard there was going to be trouble at the Jessups' farm.

"The inspectors," Doc Robertson, who was holding his whip and waiting for his gray mare, had said, "will be up on the seven o'clock train."

"The durned cusses won't like it," said Tim O'Malley, who just hung around places, mostly the blacksmith shop.

"They'll have to abide by the law," said Doc Robertson sharply.

" 'Tis said," said Tim O'Malley, crossing his knees on an old anvil, "that between them, they'd have guns."

Theodore meant to see this if he never saw anything else for the rest of his life. The Jessup boys standing off the government men with guns! He had great sympathy with them. The inspectors were probably coming to order the Jessup boys around. There was enough of that already, he thought, in this world.

He strode across Aunt Charlotte's side lawn, making green footprints on the crystal of the September dew. When he noticed how nice they were, he could not help stooping to give the grass one wide, sweeping pass with his hand, and after that he went directly up the gravel of Grandfather's drive. Here, he had time to pull something out of his pocket. It was a piece of rumpled paper with some writing on it. "Sweet Auburn," it said, "loveliest village of the plain." He looked at it once and put it in his pocket again. Nobody was ever going to know he had *that*. For quite a while it had been in a hole in his mattress, but today, because he was going away, he would have to find a safer place to hide it. He could not risk its being discovered by any female.

In Grandfather's kitchen garden, though he kept in mind that he must not waste too much time, Theodore could not help making a little snare for Old Toomey. It was only a few rocks and sticks pushed hurriedly together, but he hoped Toomey would trip over them and fall flat on his face in what was left of the row of string beans. It was not a particular revenge, but just because Toomey was the worst of all the family gardeners. George Morris, *Mister* George Morris, at Uncle Warren's was bad enough. He

used a dog and a whip in the strawberry season, and his
screeching little girl as well, but Old Toomey would hardly
grow anything for fear someone might eat it. Theodore
drew a thread of tomato vine neatly over the snare.

At the end of Grandfather's he crossed the swamp by
striding from tuft to tuft. He sometimes seemed to be im-
ploring heaven for something with his arms in the air, but
he kept his balance and did not fall in. At the swamp's
farther end was one tall pine tree. There was a squirrels'
nest at the top. He and Hubert had got a baby squirrel out
of it in the spring and had taken the best of care of it too,
until Aunt Charlotte had come over one day. Of course,
sitting on the piazza gossiping, she had rocked on it. She
was a woman, it seemed to Theodore, who scarcely knew
the difference between right and wrong. He climbed the
tree now, took his poem out of his pocket, laid it carefully
in the squirrels' nest, and put some green needles on top
to hold it down. He felt greatly relieved. It seemed just the
right place for it until he came back, and the thought
made him so energetic that he climbed the hill that ran
off to the right so that he could visit a foxhole at the top.
It was a good foxhole, fresh and strong, and as he was on
his stomach already, he rolled once or twice in the fresh
wet grass. Then he single-footed down to the Hammonds'
barn, where he went in and softly punched the work
horses on their noses. That was enough. He must seriously
now get on with business, so jogging, he turned down to
the main road, crossed it, and went up the Reservoir until
he came to the slope that looked down on the Jessups'

farm. This he climbed from the back and near the top walked on his knees to the stone wall that divided the hill in two. He pulled a stone out of place and looked through. The Jessups were there all right. He could see at least three of them on the front piazza, sitting with their chairs tipped back against the wall and their feet on the rungs, just sitting at this time in the morning. There wasn't, he noticed, a cow to be seen. It looked pretty queer. It was after milking time, and the cows should have been streaming out into the pastures, and the men should have been in the barns cleaning up. He could see by the side of the road the platform where the big cans stood to be taken away. It was full, so the milk was ready. And there was another queer thing. Not one of the Jessups' dogs was loose. Then he saw the queerest thing of all. Coming up the main road, which was just below him, was one of Mr. Silas Hawkins' black cabs, with his slow old chestnut horse, and Mr. Hawkins, who kept the livery stable and met trains, was on the box. His mustache was as plain as day, and Theodore had a chance to see it distinctly, because the slow old horse was going slower than ever before in his life. Although Theodore had had no breakfast, he felt his insides expand. He was born lucky that was all! He could bet one of his lives that inside the cab were the government inspectors, and if there was going to be trouble, he was just in time to see it all.

The first thing he saw was that Mr. Hawkins' old horse stopped dead. There seemed no reason for it except that Mr. Hawkins himself wanted to look at the three men on the Jessup piazza as they turned in unison and picked up and laid over their knees whatever it was that looked like heavy sticks that had been standing beside them.

"The guns," Theodore said, between his teeth.

As he was tugging to open his shirt collar so he could breathe better, two heads stuck themselves out of opposite windows of the cab and shouted. Mr. Hawkins still looked without answering, and then slowly and carefully got down from the box and stood close to the rump of his horse. From there he chirruped and jerked the reins, and the horse began to go forward. The two inspectors popped in and out of the windows, urging him on.

"I'm agoing on," said Mr. Hawkins loudly, "but I don't like the looks er things."

Theodore put back his head until he almost fell over and laughed silently at the sky, but he was sorry afterwards that he had wasted the time. During it the Jessup boys took their first shot, and the dust of the road in front of the old horse was smoking and so was one of the guns when he looked again. The two inspectors, who had started to get out, started to get in again as fast as they could, and Mr. Hawkins had his back pressed close against the front wheel.

"This ain't to my likin'," he told the inspectors loudly.

Theodore saw the second Jessup shot. It made the old horse prick up his ears and look at the puffs of dust in front of him. Theodore could see he was wondering, and he put down his long nose to give them a sniff just when the third shot came. That made him make up his old mind. He wheeled slowly, and while he was wheeling, the inspectors tried to say things to the Jessup boys. One of them waved a badge. The Jessup boys did not answer but stood with their three guns pointing at the ground ready, and as the inspectors did not get out, the old horse decided to take them away.

Theodore forgot where he was, and he forgot what he was doing. He stood up and crowed, he flapped his wings; finally he had to get down on his knees again and yell at the grass. But in between he watched Mr. Hawkins running beside the cab and making jumps to get on the step while the old horse lolloped back down the main road and kept the cab wobbling from side to side. When Mr. Hawkins did get up on the box again, he sat down so hard his top hat flew off and bounced into the road. Theodore had to have another crow. Then he watched the Jessup boys get up, spit over the piazza railing, and saunter one behind the other off to the barns. He waited where he was until the cows came meandering out and spread themselves over their meadows.

On the way home Theodore stopped to call on Uncle Charles. He was entitled, he thought, to a good breakfast. Not just porridge, eggs, bacon, toast, jam, and milk as they had at the Red House every morning, but perhaps pancakes with hunks of butter and drenched with maple syrup. He wanted a feast as a celebration. Big Nora, who was in Uncle Charles's kitchen, said she had second sight for anyone who was coming. Uncle Charles, however, was surprised to see him and opened his eyes and mouth and fiddled with his watch chain.

"Smell get all the way down to your house?" he asked insultingly.

But Theodore was not going to be insulted. He seemed to light up all over, skin, freckles, eyes, eyebrows, and hair. "Pancakes?" he said meekly.

"I shouldn't be surprised," said Uncle Charles. "That is, if you can endure the use of a little soap and water. How," he added, looking truly amazed, "do you Cares manage it so early in the morning?"

"I just went for a little walk," said Theodore, trying to straighten himself out quickly.

"Well, walk into the bathroom," said Uncle Charles.

When Theodore started home again through Uncle Charles's apple orchard, he had his hands in his pockets and his head in the air. He often walked this way when he had to think. It was too bad Jane and Hubert were always so sure he was trying to smell something bad. Never mind them, now he had to think. Uncle Charles had not only given him pancakes, but a lot of advice as well. And a lot more advice when he told him about the Jessup boys getting the government men on the run.

"The Jessup boys are a pack of fools," Uncle Charles had said. "The men will be back. You can't beat the government."

Theodore had wanted to know with the utmost politeness if the government was going to take the whole of Summerton and do what it liked with it.

"Did you ever go into the Jessups' barns?" Uncle Charles inquired. "Cesspools!" he had added to his pancakes.

But it was not dirt, Theodore found out, that the government men were objecting to. It was hoof-and-mouth disease. The hoof-and-mouth disease was a bad thing all right, he had to acknowledge. They did not have it on the family farms, and they did not want it either. But the government had no consideration. A lot of the farmers believed they had no judgment either. They came into a barn and said the cows must be killed—a man's whole herd. Theodore had heard the farmers talking. At the blacksmith shop in spite of the blacksmith's bad temper you could hear almost anything if you did not look as if you were listening. "Them cows don't look bad, they don't act bad. Sure there was one old milker last week that was kinder ailing. We gut rid of her like we was told to. They ain't paid us nothin' yet."

Jake Jessup and his two brothers had been the most angry. They had said some things that made Theodore feel as if he was on fire.

"They don't take the rich men's cows, we'll stake our heads on that."

Jeff and Adeniram Jessup had nodded their heads. They might have flicked a look in Theodore's direction, but he was examining some old horseshoes.

The Jessups were sure the government men didn't know what they were doing. "Pink-faced rats that are bin to school and never seen a farm," Adeniram said. "They ain't give a thought to what the poor kin eat."

Theodore had refused a third helping of pancakes at Uncle Charles's reluctantly, but suddenly. This was what no one had thought of. If all their cows were killed, how would the Jessups eat? Although the inspectors had been so funny, Theodore now saw that they were dangerous. And that someone would have to do something, somebody who *realized*. The Jessups, even if they were a little shift-less, were good people. He could swear to that. They were the best hunters and fishermen in town. Miss Jessup, their sister, was the most generous female he had ever met. She often came right out to the yard when he was on Cinder with a piece of cake. Old Mrs. Jessup was not a bad old crone either. She had only one tooth and about a dozen cats, but she never interfered with anybody, and whatever you said to her made her cackle. It often made him feel as witty as hops. Why should people like this, Theodore asked the horizon to tell him, have to be starved out by two pip-squeak government men who came to see them in one of Mr. Hawkins' cabs.

As he reached the Red House and went up the stone steps to the porch two at a time, Theodore had thought of such a good, easy, simple plan to rescue the Jessups that he wondered if pancakes had a good effect on the brain. He regretted not taking a third helping. To hops with it! He had never been stronger. And all he had to do was get out his pony, go round the back way to the Jessups' mead-ows, and somewhere take down a fence or two, or a wall, and let the cows out. When the inspectors came back, they would all have disappeared. It was so easy.

But he found it was not quite so easy as he had thought. Cinder was in fine shape. She was in almost too fine shape, he discovered, to want to stand by a gate or in the underbrush while he struggled with stones and bars. He had to do things in a hurry because some of the fences were near a road, and he had to pull things down with only one hand because of the bridle over his other arm. It was a terrible job. He grew so hot he could feel himself almost smoking. And he grew so anxious and furious, he hated even the Jessup boys for getting themselves into so much trouble. In the end, however, he managed to make three good gaps, and when he got into the saddle again, he was much pleased to see that several cows had raised their heads already and were looking interestedly in his direction. You could trust cows! They would always get out if you gave them the least chance. He cantered round the base of a grassy hill to the pasture where he knew the Jessups let their heifers run in the fall. That was safe and easy. He just slipped the top bar off the gateway. Any heifer would be glad to jump the other two. On the way home he swung round by the Twenty Acre Lot at the back of Aunt Charlotte's woods, and there he let Cinder out and himself too. Let the inspectors come back with the whole United States Army, if they wanted. They would have to prance all over Summerton to find the Jessups' herd. As he pulled Cinder up to cool her off, this idea made him tip back his head and laugh again at the sky.

He was late for lunch. He had to apologize to his stepmother. That was a rule Father had made. But he did it out loud to her face, not mumbling into his napkin. Why be meeching, when he knew what he had done for his friends? It was almost like saving the guys' lives. Everything, he felt sure, was going to be all right.

A little later Theodore saw that he had made one mistake. He should have remembered something. Because he hadn't, Hubert's asininity nearly fixed him.

Like all kids, Theodore had noticed, Hubert every now and then got stuck on something. (He could remember doing it himself.) And just now Hubert was stuck on moles. He wasted his time for hours every day going round on his hands and knees all over the front and back yards following mole runs. It was no good showing him it was senseless; he liked to do it. And he got encouragement because every once in a while he caught up with a mole and was able to transport it out through the carriage-house drive to the pony paddock and the Big Field and let it go. He felt he was benefiting the human race in spite of what Nurse said about the knees of his pants.

It was while he was doing this to what he described as a wonderful fresh run on the front lawn, where he had tracked the mole to the edge of the wall that held the lawn back from the road, that he had felt something warm on the back of his neck. He thought, he said later, that Jane had been following him, and he told her to stop breathing on him. He said he was busy. When he had heard a loud sigh, he had looked up and found that what was breathing on him was not Jane, but what Theodore had forgotten, the big face of the Jessups' bull. Hubert confessed that he knew the bull very well and that he had been told many times that he wouldn't hurt a flea. In spite of this, he had not waited to see but had run like a steam pump for the front door and rolled in. Luckily Theodore himself had been in the front hall digesting his lunch, and Jane had been there too in her riding clothes, ready to go out. In fact, Hubert ran into Jane, which she had objected to, saying his teeth had dented her leg. But worse than this, Madam had been standing on the stair landing just going up to take her afternoon's rest, and she had paused to see if anything was the matter. Ted had to hand it to Hubert that he had had a little nerve at just the right time. "I stumbled," Hubert said, smiling weakly at Madam and rubbing his elbow. So, as there was nothing wrong, Madam went on upstairs. Then Hubert told them if they wanted to see something, they better look out the window.

"Flaming spikes!" said Theodore, after he had looked.

The bull was not doing anything and he did not seem angry, but a sniff of Hubert had certainly made him curious. He was putting up his head and spreading his nostrils. Presently he opened his mouth, and a great round mournful bellow came out. Perhaps it was the luckiest thing of the whole day that Nurse had come down to get Edie a while ago and she was supposed to be taking her nap. Still, a couple of noises like that would certainly make her curious too. But for a few minutes Theodore could only stare.

"He thinks you're a cow, I guess," said Jane.

"I hope he won't try coming in to find out," said Hubert, going to shut the front door hard.

As soon as he heard the slam, the bull began pawing and tossing his head. They were all awe-struck, but Theodore realized finally what absolutely had to be done.

"We'll have to do something," he said suddenly and violently.

Jane and Hubert did not answer. There was nothing they particularly wanted to do except stay in the house.

"We can't let him go down to the village."

"Why not? Somebody's sure to see him."

"That's just it," said Theodore. "That's exactly it."

He couldn't listen to anything they said. He knew they must all go out the back way, saddle up, and chase the bull back up the main road.

Jane thought they ought to tell somebody. Probably Pat was in the barn polishing bridles.

"No!" said Theodore, shaking his finger under her nose. "No!"

He could hardly believe it, but even though he called them old women, cowards, sissies, babies, and ghouls, they still hung back.

"All right," he said, "I'm going. You can see me gored if you like right before your eyes."

"I don't think more than one of us ought to be gored at a time anyway," said Hubert, taking another look at the bull. But Jane gave in slowly and reluctantly. She did get started.

With such a pair of helpers Theodore didn't know that he had ever had such a hard time getting something accomplished. The bull did not want to go home; he wanted to see the world. Before he would turn, they had to charge him, and the helpers were not any Light Brigade. As Theodore was ready to give the word of command, Hubert wanted to know what a bull did. "Does he stick his horns in you," he asked, "or just toss you up in the air?"

"Both," said Jane, taking the guts out of everything.

By yelling and his own good generalship alone, Theodore felt, they finally got the bull started back. But there was more trouble at Aunt Charlotte's corner. The bull decided that Aunt Charlotte's lawn was better than anything he had seen for a long time. It took a crack with a riding crop to send him waddling across Grandfather's and up toward the Hammonds'. The helpers by some miracle stood where they were meant to and even made some small unenergetic maneuvers to keep him from turning back to the village. Once started on the right track they were able to walk behind him like a well-drilled company of cavalry, gently but firmly reminding him to keep on, until he caught sight of his own meadows. Then he blew through his nose and walked faster. Theodore stopped his cavalry with a raised hand.

"He's near enough now," he said, as they watched the bull amble into a trot down the Hammonds' hill. "Phew," he added, wiping his sleeve across his face. "That was a close shave."

"We'd better let somebody know," Jane had to say again.

But there was no one in sight. The whole of Summerton was as deserted as the moon all that afternoon.

Theodore said "sh" unnecessarily. "Just sh. Before you get garrulous, old girl, you'd better come home."

Jane would hush if he wanted, but she wasn't coming home. She meant to finish her ride.

"All right," said Theodore, "go ahead, but you'd better remember what's good for you. 'Hear no evil, see no evil, speak no evil.'"

"What do you mean by that sage advice?" asked Jane, turning her pony.

"Sh," said Theodore, putting his finger to his lips. "Just what I say, that's all, and you'll live to grow up and get married. Come on, Hubert."

Jane turned right through the Hammonds' barnyard and across the fields to Aunt Charlotte's woods, taking a long slow ride, a complete circle on the good clay roads. In the end she climbed the hill that brought her out at the top of the Twenty Acre Lot. She wanted to survey the countryside and see it all—the spires of the church in one direction and all the farms, cupped in green velvet, in the other. As far as she could tell, she had not seen any evil or heard any evil anywhere, but what she did see and hear was the whole of the Jessups' herd of cows meandering slowly and lowingly back to their barns to be milked. Some of them were a good ways away, she thought, but they were all coming. They looked wonderful from where she was, but she would not have dreamed of speaking of so pretty a sight when she got home. Anyway, there was no one to speak to about it. The boys were not there and did not come in until almost dark.

Theodore and Hubert had watched Jane out of sight and then gone in the other direction. They could, Theodore suggested, have one last ride through the Milldale pastures. He did not feel he had to mention it to Hubert, but things had gone so well he did not want to disturb them. The Milldale pastures were on the other side of the Reservoir basins, land and water and hills and lanes away from any questions about loose bulls. Besides, the pastures were the place to be on an afternoon like this. They were the color of an old chestnut bur by this time, and the ground was springy. Hubert had been willing and so for once had his pony, Old Tom Jones, so they had gone larking over every wall from Summerton to Canboro and then back again to the Sewertax Gate. Theodore commanded that they come out over its three bars into the lane that led to the Milldale dairy.

"You pick up my bones," was all Hubert had said.

"I will," Theodore answered generously.

They both made it. Cinder flew from start to finish. Tom Jones scampered, stopped short as if he were going to refuse, and then gave a gigantic hop like a jack rabbit. Hubert was still there as he scampered on down the lane.

On the way home they did not try to ride correctly. They let their reins lie loose and lounged in the saddle. Theodore was proud of everything, himself, Hubert, their ponies, the misty blue dusk. They had done everything as well as they could. Going past the farmhouse door, they had to bow to Milldale Smith who was in a rocking chair on the piazza.

"Just waiting here to get the undertaker," he said to them in reply.

As soon as they were on the road again, they looked at each other and smiled.

It was Edie who got and spread the news. Edie was often as good as a newspaper, especially in the evening. She would go in and stand by Nurse's elbow during the kitchen supper and keep very quiet. That was all she had to do. Tonight she came into the library, where Jane and the boys had settled themselves as soon as they found that Madam had guests in the Rose Parlor, and she looked, they saw, glancing over the tops of their books, as if she were wagging her tail. It was the very kind of time to ignore her. But she would not settle down or even tease Bing, Madam's fox terrier, who had been brought into the library with them to be out of the way too; she had to walk round and round. As this did not do her any good, she walked across the sofa and the window seat and Father's desk. After that she began walking over people's feet. It was a temptation that Theodore could not resist. Just at the right time he lifted his foot. Edie came down with a crash.

It took a long time to straighten out who was really to blame, and the news was nearly forgotten, but not quite. Just as Theodore was stretching his hardest with his book in the air and his mouth open, she said clearly: "The cows got put in."

"What cows?" said Theodore, collapsing suddenly from his stretch.

"The ones that were out," said Edie. *"I* don't know."

"Do you know that or are you lying?"

Edie retreated backwards and got her hair out of her mouth. "And," she said, "they are going to kill them every one. You're the lie teller. Why didn't you take me this morning?"

Theodore put his book carefully face down on the table as if he were anxious to keep the place, gave another half-stretch, said he'd better get ready for dinner, and walked as slowly as he was able out the door. In the hall he almost knocked down and ran over two of Madam's guests who were saying good-by. He had to make up for it. He had to stop and bow and apologize and shake hands and answer questions until he thought his head would fly off. But at the door he took the opportunity to slip out after them as if he were still being polite. His back almost wrinkled for fear it would hear Madam's voice. She would be asking him where he was going so soon before dinner. Naturally he could not explain. He doubted at the moment whether there was anyone in the world with intelligence enough to understand why he had to get back to the Jessups' farm. And of one thing he was sure. There was no one like that in his own family. But he had to go even if he was killed for doing it. He jumped the steps to the drive and ran to the carriage house for his bike. There was a little trouble, as usual, with his acetylene lamp, but it began to work finally, and just as he saw the lamps of the democrat

wagon bringing Father from the station, he was ready to
fly out the circular drive. It was bad luck that he was seen
by Father. It meant he had to wait. Father thought that
whatever he had to do could be done after dinner just as
well.

"It's just a short errand," Theodore said. "I'll be right
back."

Father simply took his arm and headed him up the
steps. "Damn!" said Theodore under his breath.

"No swearing," said Father. "I'm hungry, old chap."

Theodore had never sat through so terrible a dinner. It
was not only that Jane and Hubert took two helps of everything, but Edie had one of her chewing nights. Although
the roast lamb, in Theodore's opinion, was tender enough
to go down whole, Edie chewed and chewed and chewed.
In the end she had to be led out to the pantry by Gander,
and he refused to think about what happened to her there;
it wasn't important. It was only important that hours went
by while they waited. And then it had to be cherries for
dessert. Edie carefully took out every stone. When he asked
her kindly if she had to be so slow, she accused him of saying a tree would sprout in her stomach if she ever swallowed a stone. Theodore really wondered why he did not
go off like a stick of dynamite. It would have served her
right.

But perhaps it helped him. As he came out to get his
bicycle, which was leaning against the post of the porte-
cochère, there was an enormous orange moon coming up
over the Big Field, and he saw that if he were careful he

would not have to struggle again with the acetylene lamp. He got on and, peering hard, pumped up the dim white road.

When Theodore got to the top of the hill where he had been that morning, the Jessup house and barns were unlit black shapes. So they must be all right. He did not know what he thought might have happened to them, but he was glad to see they were all right. There was a lot going on, however. The meadow between and behind the house and barns was alive with moving men. He could see them because of a tremendous bonfire and because a lot of them held lanterns and flares. Somewhere behind the bonfire there was what looked like a long black river that he could not remember had been there before. He looked behind him quickly to be sure the Reservoir basin was in the right place. And then someone threw on more wood, and the firelight flared. He saw that the river was empty and had raw clay sides. It was a tremendous ditch. *What* was going on?

At the sound of a shot his heart gave a jump of delight and relief. Whatever it was, the Jessup boys, he was sure, were going to defend themselves to the death. He expected to see the men at the bonfire and ditch disperse, but instead the crowd closed up for a moment and then opened out again and waited. There was another shot. The crowd looked like a concertina the way it opened and shut, Theodore thought, before it jumped into his mind what the reason was. He had to bend over as if he had been hit in the stomach. He was not sick, but he wanted to be so much that he had to squeeze his ribs to stop it. He saw, he knew, that the inspectors had come back with a lot of men— maybe some of them were soldiers—and they were killing the Jessups' cows. When a cow was shot, they pushed her in the ditch. The torches flared all over the field and so did the bonfire, but not any hotter or brighter than Theodore when he could let his ribs go. Holy, holy, how he hated everybody but the Jessups. What could he do for them? They were probably inside the black house listening. They were probably thinking of their poor decrepit old cows.

Theodore certainly did not pray, but he did clench his hands at the sky. While he was doing it, he thought of something. He thought of what Pat had said one day when they met Mick Masters coming out of the saloon. "He's after having a wee bit of something to salvage his heart." That's what the Jessups must need all right.

He rode home standing half out of the saddle of his bike to get better speed. He did not care or even watch for ruts or stones but held the handle bars as if they were Cinder's reins and kept them in order the same way. He didn't know what the hurry was, but he was sure he must get back as soon as he could.

For a living wonder there was no one in the hall or the dining room when he came in—oh yes, there was—Jane. His dear sister Jane had chosen this night of all nights to make an enormous drawing on the dining-room table. Worse than that, as he stopped and drew in his breath, he could hear that Gander was still in the pantry smashing dishes around. Theodore took hold of all his muscles and then leaned on the table opposite Jane. "You've *got* to help me this time," he said. In spite of all he could do, he could not keep his fist from kneading the table. Jane looked up. And she looked at his fist. For once her female nature did not make her ask "what for?" Instead she looked at him hard for another minute. "How?" she said.

"Get her out of there," said Theodore, motioning toward the pantry. His voice, he thought, must have been affected by bicycling so hard.

Jane got up. "You'll have to give me time," she said, "till I can get down cellar."

Theodore swallowed and nodded.

Jane was quicker than he had thought she could be. Before he had walked around the table three times, he could hear her voice wailing. Gander came into the dining room, wiping her hands on a dish towel. "The saints preserve us," she said. "What are you after wanting now?"

"It's not me," said Theodore innocently. "It sounds like Jane in the cellar."

"Whisht," said Gander, disappearing.

The minute he heard the second door fall to, he tiptoed into the pantry, went down on one knee, and opened Father's wine closet. He took out a full bottle that said "Dewars" on the label and slipped it under his coat. He met Jane, who had come out the back way, under the porte-cochère.

"I don't see what you're in such a hurry for," she said. "Are you going to drink the whole bottle yourself?"

"Go away," said Theodore. "Just go away, will you?"

He was sorry when he tried to get on his bicycle again that he had not asked her to stay. Carrying a bottle was no joke. When he almost let it drop on the hard-packed drive, he felt as if he were turned to ice, and when at last he got it buttoned inside his shirt, he was streaming with sweat. It was all uphill to the Jessups', and Theodore pumped till he thought his heart and arms would come out. This time he did not branch off to go to the hill but rode straight up the road. No one was on it and no one was around the front of the farmhouse when he got there. The bonfire was still going and so were the shots and the concertina, but he did not look too carefully. He did not want to see a whole lot more. He dumped his bicycle in the grass directly opposite the dark farmhouse and crossed the road. Then in the good safe darkness, where the trees hid the moon, he walked along the house side to the kitchen door. Tiptoeing up the two steps, he carefully fished inside his shirt for the bottle and carefully and quietly stood it on the door tread. He felt to see if it were perfectly steady, and then he backed noiselessly away. But he found he could not back far enough. His heel hit something hard, and when he lost his balance, he reeled against something soft.

"I caught cher at it," a man's voice said.

It did not occur to Theodore that someone might think he'd been stealing, but it did occur to him that he had been caught doing something he would never know how to explain. He convulsed himself like an eel and turned at the same time. The man made a grab, but Theodore made a jerk and got away. He ran stumbling and tripping, but faster than any grown man could run, to where his bicycle lay. He picked it up, panting, and glanced toward the house. It was Jake who was there and had found the bottle. Theodore could only hope he had not seen his face. Even in the dark it seemed to be getting red. Just the same he had to watch a little longer. Jake held the bottle up and tried to look at it by the reflected light of the bonfire, and Theodore was almost sure that when he saw what it was, he would feel better. Theodore started to get on his bicycle but stopped, frozen dead. Jake was taking the bottle by the neck and was drawing back his arm. The next minute he had hurled it into the air. Theodore could not see it flying up or down, but he heard it land short of the road and smash to bits. Then Jake opened the door and went into the dark house.

Theodore walked his bicycle part-way home. He wanted more night air on his face so that it would stop feeling stiff and hot. Opposite the swamp behind Grandfather's, he sat on the wall for a while to get a rest, and when he felt strong enough, he crossed the swamp to the big pine tree, climbed it by the help of the moon, got his poem out of the squirrels' nest, put it in his pocket, and came down. He did not try to look at it. He took it away because the place was not safe any more. Was anyplace in Summerton safe? For the last part of the way he rode, jolting with care now over the gravel. He did not choose to go in the front door. Someone, he thought, would be sure to be around. He did not choose to see anyone at present. He had not wanted to go to boarding school, but now he thought that perhaps it was not such a bad idea. He better find out how things really were in the world so that he would not make such bad mistakes. He circled the house to see where the family was, and, finding that only Jane's room was dark, he decided to climb up her wisteria vine and go in her window. His own room was full of light, and there were two women in it—Nurse and Gander probably stirring up his clothes to get them ready for packing.

Jane's door was open when Theodore stepped through the window and stood listening so that he would know what was going on in the rest of the house. By the light from it he could see her bed with no one in it, clothes she had not picked up on a chair, and on her mantelpiece the glint of a silver box. That silver box was where Jane kept her private papers. He knew because he had once looked. He listened with all his might. He was safe, he thought, for at least a few minutes. Stepping softly over to the mantelpiece, he opened the silver box, scrabbled up the loose papers in it with one hand, and with the other laid his poem neatly on the bottom. Then he put Jane's things back on top of it and closed the lid. The poem was printed, and it had no name on it. It would probably be all right there for a thousand years.

When he stepped out into the hall, he walked across the head of the stairs and along to his own door. He would have to get those females out of there somehow, because he was now so tired it was hard to stand up.

"If you don't mind," he said politely to Nurse and Gander, who were gossiping with some of his clothes in their hands, "I would like my room now. Would you please get out."

"We're just afther putting you to rights, Master Theodore," said Gander, but she did not stop with the story she was telling Nurse.

"Would you *please*," began Theodore even more politely, but suddenly Nurse's and Gander's female faces became too much for him. "Get out of my room," he shouted. "Decamp, vamoose, skiddoo, GET OUT."

He did not care that the door he shut behind him slammed so that the house shook. He flung himself on his bed and put his face down as hard as he could on the hard pillow. He chewed into it until there was a hole, and when the feathers began to come out, he banged it over and over with his fist. The world was so un-understandable that he would like to punch it to death. Suddenly he rolled over flinging out his arms and legs, and in one more minute he was asleep.

CHAPTER TWO

Hubert's Lamb

Of all mean things that had ever been done to anybody, Jane thought, Father had done the worst to her when he got the idea that she had no education.

"You know a lot of things, Jane," Hubert had said sadly, after this had been discovered, "but I guess they're not the right ones."

The disaster had come about because, although Jane could remember her red arithmetic book perfectly plainly, she could not make out the table of pints, quarts, and gallons on the fourteenth page when Father inquired about them. So they had all—Madam, Theodore, who still had a few more days at home, Hubert and Edie—had to listen while they were eating roast chicken at dinner one evening to Jane, at bay, saying not only to arithmetic, but then through the whole range of history, geography, and grammar, that she did not know. It was what Theodore afterwards described as "the most terrible exposure of ignorance in modern times."

As usual Ted was only being superior so Jane could not bother about him. Nor did she mind either not knowing where Venezuela was—who would care, if they lived a hundred years?—but her not knowing gave Father an idea. Everything in the Red House had improved since Madam came, especially Father, but even she could not keep him from having ideas. And Father's ideas were mostly frightful. This one broke his record. Even Hubert thought so, and he had followed Jane round the carriage-house yard, where she had gone in the dark to try to find some stones to kick, trying to be consoling. Because it had turned out that instead of going to Miss Lincoln's school in the village, which they had all done since they could remember—a good school that smelled of the cookies Miss Lincoln baked three times a week, and where there was a parrot on the back porch—Jane was to stay at home this winter and have a governess.

"Me!" Jane had said, turning to her stepmother at the end of the table.

She found it sickening suddenly to realize that there was no use telling anybody that she knew how to throw green apples nearly as well as Theodore and that she could box better, much better, than Hubert.

"Don't you want to learn something, Janey?" her stepmother had asked.

It was simply no use saying, as she explained to Hubert, that she knew everything already. Hubert nodded, even though she could not see him. He understood her perfectly.

"Besides," he said, "she can't be very educated herself. She's too nice."

But Jane was not going to be put off the track by Madam's niceness, not this time. Madam had agreed with Fa-

ther about a governess, and Jane was shocked. She urgently
wanted someone to know that what she knew *were* the
right things. Didn't she know all about the Red House
from start to finish, its animals alive and dead, the trap
door in the cellar, all the roads in Summerton, the happen-
ings on the family dairy farms—hadn't she seen a calf born
a week ago? Did he remember she could almost milk? She
knew how to catch muskrats in the Reservoir basins; she
knew what to do when chased by heifers; she knew how to
steal strawberries out of the family gardens, climb trees,
skin squirrels, use a slingshot, and ride Chris over the stee-
plechase course set up by Theodore in the Milldale pastures.
What else did a person need in life? Did he remember she
could jump the Sewertax Gate?

"I can beat you at croquet," said Jane. "I once saw a
dead man, remember? Will Crouch in his coffin. I was
nearly dead myself the day I fell in the reservoir dam."

Hubert knew it all and was impressed.

"Are you sure they said a *governess?*" he asked, hardly
able to believe it himself. He was so glad it wasn't him that
he wanted to stand on his head. There *was* no consolation
that he could see.

"If you're not deaf, you heard what they said," said Jane
crossly. "How do I know what kind?"

Hubert took one more try. "I suppose at least we could
try to get rid of her," he said at last, consideringly.

But Jane would not take him seriously. She couldn't see
him bodily removing a governess, she said frankly, even a
small one, and she didn't know if he was bright enough to

think of anything else. She went off and left him. If she was going to be tracked round by a keeper for the rest of her life, she had better, she felt, take her shame into the still deeper darkness of the fields.

Hubert went back to the house worried. The thought of a perpetual teacher in the house made him shudder, not only for Jane. He interrupted Theodore, who was lacing a football in the front hall, and asked him about it.

"Yep," said Theodore, "she'll be a hag of every description. They always are."

He also said definitely, as soon as he did not have to hold the lace in his teeth, that Hubert should leave matters alone. "It's an affair for the women, old man," he said. "Stay away from it. It won't hurt the wild cat to tame her a bit."

After this it was clear to Hubert that Jane was left without a friend in the world except himself, and he could think of but one remedy. There were lots of ways, he thought, to get rid of governesses, if they really tried. But Jane had no confidence.

"She hasn't even come yet," was all she would say gloomily.

The children were not sent to the station to meet Mademoiselle; they were not even told that she was on the way. They came in from a ride one afternoon and there she was, nosing like a large black elephant into a bureau drawer in Jane's own room. Jane turned about without a word and walked away. Theodore and Hubert would have done the same, but the elephant straightened up and turned around and found them staring at her. They had to shake hands and tell her their names before they could get away.

"M'sieur 'Uber,' and M'sieur T-e-odorr, I underrrstand," said Mademoiselle.

Theodore ran as hard as Hubert after they had stalked dignifiedly out of sight, but he had to be awfully funny about it afterwards.

"MOOseer, OOO Bear, you're going to spend the winter with a living tombstone," he delighted himself saying. "Mark my words."

All Hubert could say back was "Not if I know it," and wag his head. But Jane knew this was the vain, vain boasting that Hubert sometimes did, and she knew it was even vainer when Theodore brought back his report from the kitchen. He had gone out there to get something to sustain him after seeing Mademoiselle and had noticed that the stove was perfectly bare at a time when there should have been a lot of steaming pots and pans.

"No dinner tonight?" he asked Cook, trying to be jovial.

" 'Tis eggs, your honor," said Cook.

"So we eat with the obelisk," he reported to Jane and Hubert in the library, where they felt Mademoiselle would not dare to come so soon. "Alone."

As usual they would not believe him until they came downstairs to the red and white hall and found Father and Madam in their best clothes standing in front of the fireplace. They were waiting to say good night before they went out. Mademoiselle's back, they also saw, was in the dining room already, sitting in Father's chair. And Edie—Edie, on one of the Rose Parlor cushions—was pulled up beside her in reach of her large left hand. It was as good a sight, Theodore thought, as he had seen in a long time, but Jane and Hubert felt they were looking at what Nurse called "an omen." And it was they who turned out to be right. Mademoiselle began doing things at once. She began to pray out loud at table just as if she were a clergyman, and after that was over she unfurled her napkin like a sail and tucked one corner of it into her collar. No one wished to say a word or even look. They had seen something even worse. Mademoiselle had a black mustache, and at one corner of it was a mole with a few stiff hairs.

"The better to kiss you with, my dear," said Theodore to his plate so that Jane could hear. Jane kicked him so hard under the table that his fork was jarred and his mouthful went on the tablecloth, so he used his elbow on Jane's right arm and her mouthful sprang onto the floor.

"Have you trouble with your eatings there?" asked Mademoiselle.

She was distracted just in time. Hubert decided suddenly that this might be a good time to be interested in his warts. He showed them to Edie.

"Take it away," said Edie loudly, holding her nose.

"They don't smell, goat," said Hubert, in a violent whisper. He examined his knuckles intently and then looked at Mademoiselle.

"What have you, 'Uber'?" Mademoiselle asked.

"Just a wart," said Hubert modestly, holding it out to her.

Mademoiselle craned her neck. "A 'orrid sight, certainly," she said. "Put it down."

Hubert withdrew his hand under the table as Theodore stretched to see too, and then generously took it out again to hold across to him. "Just a plain wart," said Theodore contemptuously. "I've had them myself. But you'll have to bury a cat by the light of the moon," he added.

"Iz zis what you call a tale for old wife's," said Mademoiselle. "Iz zis not?"

"How do I get warts?" asked Hubert to the world at large, but ending politely with Mademoiselle.

"Toads," said Theodore.

"An-other old wife's story, certainly," said Mademoiselle. She was doing her best to get into the conversation, Jane saw, but she didn't know the boys.

"Then it must be bad blood," said Theodore professionally. "You need to be purified. Sulphur and molasses, old boy, taken three times a day. I dare say they're good for worms, too, if you have them and you probably have." He put in a large piece of toast covered with scrambled egg.

"What is that you say Teodor?" asked Mademoiselle.

Theodore could only point to his mouth.

Hubert examined both hands. "Quite a nice crop," he said complacently.

"I had a wart once," said Theodore, swallowing his mouthful, "that I bit off and it never came back. You can try that if you like."

"It would be a regular dinner," said Hubert thoughtfully. "Mine would. I better save them for an emergency." He crouched over his plate seriously.

"That is enough about wahrts, 'Uber'," said Mademoiselle, sitting back. " 'Uber', raise yourself!" She squared her own shoulders. "Tomorrow at your studies, you must be like a sol-jair."

After this remark, Hubert was no longer interested in warts certainly. Nor in eggs either. Theodore and Jane's heads came up cautiously to look at him. He was not raising himself; he was crouching as low as if he had a pain.

Jane sat up herself. Hubert had been on her side. She was not going to desert him. "Hubert goes to Miss Lincoln's, you know," she said clearly. "Miss Lincoln doesn't care how we sit."

"And so I am here," said Mademoiselle, wiping her mouth. "Yes, for this reason. Tomorrow we begin to learn properly, *n'est-ce pas?*"

Not a word was uttered by anyone for the rest of supper except by Edie, who said: "Mademoiselle, your voice sounds as if it was gnaw-ring toast; why does it?" But she was ignored.

At the end of supper Mademoiselle asked them if they would not come with her and play a "little game," but backing away resolutely, they politely said "No." They went up to the boys' room and sat on the beds. At least Jane and Theodore did. Hubert got under his own and pulled pieces of the springs to make them twang. He had forgotten Jane. She was just a girl anyhow. He didn't care if he stayed there the rest of his life.

But Jane had not forgotten him. Hubert had been awfully decent, and his silence, except for the twanging, was frightful.

"Maybe we could get rid of her like you said," she said finally. "If we tried hard enough."

Theodore was willing to agree that in the few days he had left he would do anything they could suggest. He said he would even try to think of something himself.

"In the meantime," said Jane, getting a little brighter, "we could both be stupider than we are now to get her discouraged."

"Without any effort at all," said Theodore encouragingly.

The next morning Hubert had a cold. He said so, but it seemed so lucky they told him he was making it up. It was hard to tell at first because Father did not allow any sniffing or honking at table, and Hubert, although he kept his mouth slightly ajar, ate as usual. But as soon as Father was gone, he sneezed and coughed convincingly all over the hall.

"It's a real cold all right," he said when he could stop. "I feel awful. At least I think I do. Maybe I ought to be in bed."

"Arrhugh," said Theodore disrespectfully. "Just the same, make the most of it."

Hubert did not need that kind of advice, Jane was sure, as they were being herded into the Rose Parlor. And she herself felt stupid without any pretense. Imagine using Mother's sitting room, which, with the sun streaming in, had always felt and smelled exactly like spring, for a big black Frenchwoman who smelled like a closet. But she could not go as far as Hubert. When he did not know how to spell "apple" or what the three table was, she whispered

to him, while Mademoiselle was sharpening a pencil, that
he was overdoing it.

"I'b not either," said Hubert loudly. "I'b sick."

There was hardly a moment, it seemed, when he did
not have to make some kind of noise with his nose, and
when Jane saw him slip something from his pocket into
his mouth, she forgot to answer Mademoiselle at all.

"Parbleu!" said Mademoiselle. Jane felt a sharp pain in
her right ear. She batted at it and hit Mademoiselle's hand.
They would have sat staring at each other if Hubert's
mouth had not begun making noises too.

"What do you chew, 'Uber'?" asked Mademoiselle
sharply.

"A pill," said Hubert and stuck out his tongue to show
her a large pink tablet on the end of it. Jane saw that it was
the kind you could buy at the drugstore for five cents for a
long pink package. "For by cold," said Hubert, drawing
everything from the top of his head down into his throat.
Unfortunately, in this mighty breath the pill went too,
and Hubert's noises then became so terrible that Jane was
frightened. "You better hit him on the back," she said to
Mademoiselle. "I think he's choking to death." But by that
time Hubert was only gagging like Father's beagle just before he wanted to be sick. At the third gag, just like the
beagle, the pink tablet came shooting out and went clear
across the room.

"Heavens," Hubert said, grinning weakly at Jane. "Phew,
I thought I was a goner." He got up to cross the room and
put what was left of the pill delicately in the scrap basket.

"Par*don*," he said startlingly to Mademoiselle. *"C'est mon rhume."* Imagine Hubert knowing a word of French! Then Jane remembered that he and Miss Lincoln had been taking trips to Paris in a small green book. But she didn't know they had had any colds there. Anyway it subdued Mademoiselle. *"Tiens,"* she said. "He speaks."

Luckily Hubert's further knowledge of French conversation was not tested just then. It was eleven o'clock, and Madam came in carrying a plate of cookies. She had only to look at Hubert's red face to go over and put her hand on his forehead. Hubert sank his head on one arm languidly while she was doing it and breathed hard through his mouth.

"Bed, I think," Madam said. *"N'est-ce pas,* Mademoiselle?"

"As Madame thinks," said Mademoiselle, tapping a pencil up and down on her open palm and looking hard at Hubert.

Jane was left to be stupid all by herself. And she had had no idea it would be so hard to do with Mademoiselle's fingers ready to pinch her ear any minute. When at lunchtime Mademoiselle called her a "good *jeune fille"* and put her heavy arm across her shoulders, Jane shrank with dismay. She went at once to see Hubert. He was sitting up in a nice clean bed in the guest room sipping at an eggnog with foam and nutmeg on the top.

"Did you carry od the good work?" he asked, resting the eggnog on his stomach.

"She pinches!" said Jane. "How long are you going to be sick?"

"How do I know?" said Hubert, spreading out his hands and letting the eggnog balance. He felt cautiously along a wrinkle in the blankets. "But this I do know, Jane, certainly." He found his packet of pink tablets, unwound it, and poured them into the eggnog. "These pills are wonderful for a cold. Have some?"

"Ugh," said Jane and walked away in disgust. *He* wasn't going to have to spend days and days alone with Mademoiselle and her mustache. And indeed, while Hubert was enjoying poor health, Jane found the Rose Parlor almost unbearable. The clock stopped and waited between minutes, she was sure, and her efforts not to yawn over and over again were in danger, she thought, of breaking her jaw. But the shame of it was the worst. She, the rider of Black Eagle of the prairies, she, who had fought with Ethan Allen—!

Hubert's cold lasted more than a week, because after his nose was better, he developed a cough that sounded, Father said, like a voice from the tomb. It impressed his stepmother, and it seemed to impress Mademoiselle. It even impressed Hubert himself enough so that he talked to Jane about its being galloping consumption like old Mrs. Paine in the village. Jane, bearing the brunt of his absence, was not impressed.

"What's the use of doing this sort of stunt," she said. "Pretty soon they'll think you're an old woman with nerves."

That cured Hubert of galloping consumption overnight. The cough, he decided, was just an old hack, hack, hack, but he did what he could with it in the Rose Parlor, and Jane was not sure when she got him back that it was an improvement. Between the two of them, Mademoiselle who kept looking at the wood basket where there were some nice flat shingles, and Hubert who kept looking like a cow at Mademoiselle, she kept having the feeling that something terrible was liable to happen. Every once in a while in sheer desperation she paid attention and was able to give a right answer. It kept Mademoiselle quiet. And alas, it did something else. Jane could feel it coming on like the rising of water in the bathtub. Mademoiselle was getting to like her, and she began to tag her round. She wanted Jane to show her Summerton; she wanted her to take her to the farms; she asked about flowers and animals and talked about *la belle verdure*. If Jane had decided to take Chris out with the buggy, Mademoiselle would be sure to be on the steps as she rolled slowly through the porte-cochère. "And so the poor governess is left behind," she would say. Jane had to smile weakly, but she chucked to Chris just the same.

"American children have no hearts," said Mademoiselle to Hubert one morning. "No, none at all," and after that became sterner, rapping knuckles more often with her ruler and pinching ears at the slightest thing.

"Does she think that will work?" Jane asked Hubert.

"And nothing will work until she goes away," said Hubert firmly. He had just had to say *j'aime, tu aime, il aime* out loud, standing up and looking Mademoiselle right in the eye. When he whispered to Jane afterwards *"Je n'aime* her *pas,"* Mademoiselle put him in the corner face to the wall. All he could do there was count the patterns on the wallpaper in a hoarse monotonous voice. He did not think he was making much headway. He had tried getting another cold by sitting on damp stones but had only got mold on his trousers; he had tried sleeping fits; and he had tried what Theodore had advised—putting an alarm clock under the cushions of the rose sofa set for ten-thirty. But Mademoiselle had sat on it when she corrected Jane's arithmetic, and it not only did not go off after this but never ticked again. Ted had to go off to school without it. And after he had gone, things changed for the worse. Early supper became a regular thing and also conversation with Mademoiselle. If she could not be with them, she wanted to know all they had been doing. The only one who wanted to tell was Edie. So, without Ted to keep her down, Edie was allowed to chatter the whole solid meal.

"She's the most garrulous girl I ever heard," said Hubert with sad surprise.

He had become almost as sad as Jane, and he had an awfully good reason. Father unexpectedly had come home early one Wednesday afternoon to vote at the Town Hall, and Hubert on that very day had decided he knew enough for the time being and had gone chestnutting by himself. In fact, he had left the house so early that he was not found until he came sauntering back at five o'clock full of chestnuts. Later, he would not tell Jane what had happened to

him in Father's office, but he could not think of anything
new to do to Mademoiselle for almost a week. Jane thought
he had given in.

"I might have given in, Jane," he said later. "I just
might, but the Lord sent a lamb." That was another thing.
They had had to read Bible stories on Sunday nights, one
on each side of Mademoiselle on the Rose Parlor sofa.

The lamb was sent on a bright clear night in October
that was exactly right for them to go to the Main Dairy to
play hide and seek with the McEvoys. They did this often
in summer, walking the walls along the road that led
past Aunt Charlotte's and Grandfather's, over the hill to
where it dipped between meadows, and then went on up
a long sloping grade through deep tree shadows till the
lights of the scattered farm buildings began to show at the
end of the lane. Except for getting down at Aunt Charlotte's drive, they could make it the whole way on the
rough stones. They were expert wall-walkers, and they
liked this dark trip almost as well as the games themselves,
which—racing, tearing, hiding among the good barn and
night smells—were ecstasy enough. They had been a hundred times before, so there was no reason why Hubert should
not have mentioned it when they came out from their early
supper, even though Father had just come in from the
train and was there to overhear him.

"Zis time I go," said Mademoiselle, behind them.

Father heard her too and so did Madam who was coming down to greet him. There was no getting away. But
while Mademoiselle went upstairs to get her hat and cape

and gloves and rubbers and umbrella, Jane made a desperate try.

"Does she *have* to go with us?" she asked, standing directly in front of her stepmother and throwing out her hands.

"It's dark to be out on the roads alone, Janey," Madam said.

"There's Hubert," said Jane, still more desperate, though she would like to know who *he* could protect! "We always used to—"

"Jane!" said Father.

All they could do after that was fling themselves in separate chairs and wait for Mademoiselle. When she did come down, they had to let her clamp them each by a hand and start up to the Main Dairy in this shameful way. As soon as they were out of sight, however, they managed to drag away. Hubert walked backward in front of her all the way so that he could keep an eye on her, and Jane plodded behind thinking darkly of the lovely nights before she came. At the Main Dairy, without so much as an invitation, Mademoiselle marched up the piazza steps and sat down under the only light. From there she could see everything, she said. And from there her black mustache was as plain as day. Tim McEvoy asked Hubert where they got her.

"From France," said Hubert shortly.

"I should think yer dad coulda done better at home," Tim said.

It was an especially good night though, because it was so

clear and black, and it was made better by the McEvoys'
black and white terrier. He was not much of a dog; he was
not even much of a terrier, as Hubert told Jane while they
were hiding under the piazza. "His legs are too short for
one thing," he said, lying on his back and chewing the stem
of an old leaf comfortably because it was going to take a
long time to find them. But Stripes had fallen in love at
first sight with Mademoiselle and was keeping her busy.
They could hear him capering frantically round her over
their heads. "She must smell of meat," whispered Hubert.
"I wonder what kind."

"Grizzly," said Jane. She was hunched up on her knees,
peering through the side planks and listening hard. "You
better be ready to run; I think I hear them."

But what she heard was only Stripes trying to dance himself into Mademoiselle's lap.

"A fine dog, certainly," they heard Mademoiselle say to
someone. It must have been Mrs. McEvoy, because when
Mrs. McEvoy talked, you could never hear what she said,
and there was only a murmur in return.

"Love at last," said Hubert, rolling over and laughing
into the leaf mold. "And I bet she doesn't know he thinks
she's a bone." A second after that, they were flushed out of
their hiding place, and Hubert was caught because he
wasn't ready. While he was "it," he could see Stripes sitting
on Mademoiselle's knees, throwing his head back to try
and get a lap at her. He did not see how either of them
could stand it.

But Stripes was still enthusiastic about Mademoiselle when it was time to go home. He jumped and bobbed and panted about her and followed them down the road, unwilling to go back no matter how they shouted at or chased him. Tim had to come after him, pick him up, and carry him back.

"Zis little dog has a heart," said Mademoiselle.

In the darkness Jane and Hubert moved away while she was thinking about Stripes and his heart.

"Shall we go home on the walls?" asked Jane.

"You bet!" said Hubert.

There was so little light under the arched trees that they were able to see only the vague shadows of the stones, and they told each other for weeks afterwards that they were the luckiest people ever born to have come out into the open of the meadows where there was the faintest glimmer of a tiny setting moon so that they were able to see in time what was running gently down the wall in front of them. It was not far in front either. Jane stopped so suddenly that Hubert bumped his nose on her.

"Hey, you can't do that. You've broken my nose," Hubert said indignantly, crying from the blow.

Jane simply pointed.

"Gee," said Hubert.

He was looking at his lamb, but he did not then know it. It was black with white stripes and had a black-and-white bushy tail lifted straight into the air. They let the lamb trot on a minute and then easily and quietly dropped into the roadside grass and hopped across it to the road. Mademoiselle was there just behind them talking to herself in French.

"*Regardez,*" she said, when they joined her. "M'sieur Stripes, a bad dog. He has come again to take us home."

"Where?" they asked.

Mademoiselle waved at the wall with her umbrella.

"You mean *there?*" said Hubert, drawing in his breath.

"I do, certainly," said Mademoiselle. "I will command him to go back. *Regardez,* he waits."

The little trotting animal had stopped and turned its head to look at them.

"Mademoiselle," said Jane clearly and rather loud, "if I were you—" She clutched at Mademoiselle's skirt. But Hubert clutched her. "Run! Jane, run!" he said in an urgent whisper.

Mademoiselle strode forward shaking her skirt loose from Jane's hand and saying thousands of French words to Stripes as she threatened him by stabs and blows at the air. As she came nearer, the little animal moved its hind legs.

"Jane!" said Hubert, agonized, so that his knees bent and straightened. "RUN."

Far, far down the road, panting and exhausted, they slowed down to get their breaths. The little sliver of moon just at the brink of Aunt Charlotte's pasture hill was bright orange, and the air was as delicious as crisp brook water. But presently along it came just a threat, a tincture of skunk.

"How long will they have to bury her for, do you think?"

asked Hubert, hitching his trousers joyously. Although he
was looking up the road, his eyes were not dwelling on it,
but on a picture of Mademoiselle underground, her face
just above grass, while he fed her daily some cold oatmeal.
If it rained, they could put a chair over her head with Father's poncho thrown across it, and a little hot cocoa might
be a good thing. A few nights in the open air of America
would surely make her want to go back to *La Belle France.*
Jane roused him by saying that she hoped Mademoiselle
was not dead.

"Oh, no!" said Hubert. "We're not that lucky. Besides,
the smell of skunk is getting stronger. Come on; we better
go."

"We've got to go back," said Jane.

"Why?"

"We *have.*"

"If we do, we might have to be buried ourselves," said
Hubert. He did not like at all the picture of himself grass
high alongside Mademoiselle.

"They don't bury people," said Jane. "Pat made it up.
I asked the sexton once."

Hubert turned reluctantly in the direction of the Main
Dairy. "It's the most disappointing thing I ever heard in
my life," he said.

When they met Mademoiselle, she was walking toward
them with her arms outstretched. She had no hat, no cape,
no umbrella, and she looked as if she were playing blind-
man's buff.

"*Tiens,*" she said when she saw them, still keeping her

hands and arms up. "It was not a dog, that. It was a pole-cat."

Jane and Hubert escorted her on either side as far away as possible, waiting nervously for their cowardly flight to be mentioned, but Mademoiselle seemed to think only that they must have been worried about her and would be glad to hear the news of her escape.

"My *parapluie* save my life," she said. "It open."

Polecats they had also in France, she said, but never, 'nevair,' had she been attacked by one before. The attack was sudden, but in that moment the umbrella that she had been shaking for Mr. Stripes to return to his home had opened out, and the polecat had wasted his strength on that. But not all. A *soupçon* had come on the hands and arms. Therefore, she must bathe. But perhaps bathing would not be enough? Could they smell somsing?

"Yes," said Hubert, "definitely."

Far into the night Hubert found himself under the com-mand of Jane, taking care of Mademoiselle. He disap-proved at first, and then he began to like it. "She might as well be a fugitive slave," he said delightedly, because they had to hide her in the cellar at the bottom of the kitchen stairs while Hubert reconnoitered. When the way was clear, he waved them up, and Jane somehow got Mademoiselle with her outstretched arms to the top. The trail of skunk that Mademoiselle left in the kitchen was so bad that they hustled her up to the second floor and into their own bath-room—a good place for her to be because its other door opened into an inside corridor that Madam partly used as a dress closet, and this had still another door to the hall. The smell of skunk would be sealed right in. Once in the bathroom, where Mademoiselle subsided on a stool, they sighed with relief. Jane opened the window, and Hubert enthusiastically ran the bath water. But it was after this that the real work began. For an hour, they handed things through a crack in the door on the dress-closet side that they hoped would subdue the smell of Mademoiselle. Hubert knew where there was some creosote under the laundry tubs. After they had found it in the dark, they mixed it in a saucepan, strong, at the sink, and only slopping a few drops, they passed that in. Jane cut some lemons in two because she knew that Gander used them for onion on the knives. When she cut herself slightly as well, Hubert mopped up the juice and blood with the utmost care and hid the dish towel in the garbage pail. He said it didn't matter a bit; it was in such a good cause. They got some soap from the linen closet and the bottle of bay rum from Father's dressing table. Finally, before Mademoiselle would get into the bath water, Jane had to get a chemise out of Mademoiselle's bureau and bring it to her. Hubert brought her dressing gown without being asked. "I'd hate to see her naked," he said. "What shall we do now?"

"We might burn a few matches," said Jane, "outside the door. It doesn't smell so much of skunk any more, but it's almost worse."

"The very thing," said Hubert, and he managed to skin silently down the front stairs to the kitchen. He meant to get the big matchbox from the top of the stove. Those

matches had more wood on them than the little ones, and
the smoke they made after they were blown out would be
as good as the fumigating that was done after "hooping
cough." Jane waited for him uneasily. Bay rum, creosote,
soap, and skunk seemed to be seeping out all through the
upstairs. Nurse must have gone to bed unusually early or
certainly she would be spying round. Then Jane remembered she had heard voices through Gander's door. That
was lucky! She went once and peered over the banisters. It
was even luckier that there was a long hall with a curve in
it going from the front hall to the library, where Father
and Madam probably were. She did not see how she could
have stopped Mademoiselle from fighting that skunk, but
she had a feeling that Father and Madam would think she
should have tried harder.

As soon as Hubert got back, they lit and snuffed matches,
waving them here and there in the narrow dress closet
where the smells were the worst, and it was such a success
that they took more and more out of the box and lighted
them at the same time.

"It's a first-class smudge," said Hubert, much pleased.
"It'll kill anything."

"We better close the door to the hall," said Jane, "or
they'll think the house is on fire."

In the utter blackness of the dress closet they looked to
each other like fiends in a picture of hell. It was so satisfactory that Hubert, just as they heard Mademoiselle stirring
near the door, grabbed for the box to have a last grand illu-

mination. In his hurry he struck his five matches too hard, and one of the heads flew off. Jane dodged, and the flaming head lit on one of Madam's satin evening dresses that had a net overskirt. If they had not been so stricken with horror at what they had done, they could have moved fast enough to put it out. The flame did not shoot up right away, and Jane was able to grab the tulle and pull it off, but then the satin had caught and a steady bright fire crept up the dress. The sight was so frightening that they did not even move to open the door.

It was a good thing, Hubert had to acknowledge forever, that Mademoiselle just then came out of the bathroom.

"Otherwise we'd have been cooked, Jane, certainly," he said the next day when they were both in prison.

"Shut up," said Jane. "She saved our lives." It had been so frightful she never wanted to think about it again as long as she lived.

Mademoiselle had stood there, in the dressing gown Hubert had brought for her, as stupefied as themselves. She had looked at the flaming dress for what seemed a year—maybe two years—while the flame got brighter and bigger. It took her all that time to decide what to do. Then she stalked to the dress, turned it up from the bottom so the flame was inside, tore it from the hanger, carried it into the bathroom as if it was a Christmas pudding, and flung it into the bathtub. It gave a hiss and went out.

This was the first awfulness. The second was that while Jane and Hubert were looking at the soggy, charred mess, unable to speak or move or look at Mademoiselle or even at each other, the door had opened from the hall to the dress closet and there was Father.

"Have you children managed to bring a skunk into the house?" he said, before he saw what was in the bathtub.

"That was the smell that went downstairs first, I suppose," said Hubert, who, no matter how Jane felt, had to keep on talking about it.

For a minute Father had politely stopped at the door on account of seeing Mademoiselle. But he must have smelled a good deal more than skunk right away because his eyebrows went up and so did his mustache. Mademoiselle made a sweeping gesture toward the tub, and Father came in and looked.

"*M'sieur,*" Mademoiselle had said, "I have endure many things. Colds, laziness, bad brains, a polecat, *ma faute* may*be,* but I do not endure to be burn without closses, as zees, your children, plan for me."

"After we'd helped her with all that stuff too!"

If it had been the days before Madam came, Jane could never decide what might have happened. Father would probably have barked the house down at least or even in the end sent them to the Summerton jail to end on the gallows as Nurse so often predicted. But Madam *was* there, and she managed somehow to make a bargain for them. If they would tell the whole truth, Father would perhaps allow them to be fed once more on something besides bread and water and could after a while bear to see them within his sight.

The whole truth was very hard to tell and took some days to find. There was not only what they had done but what they hadn't. It had to come out in snatches, but somehow Madam had got them not exactly forgiven—there were no more allowances for weeks, that was for letting Mademoiselle get skunked; they could not ride all month, that was for playing with fire; no ice cream for Sunday dinner until Christmas, that was for stealing the bay rum ("Actually he barked loudest about that," said Hubert); slave labor in the barn for an hour every night unlimited, that was for Madam's dress—but somehow she did fix it so that at least they were able to leave their rooms and join the human race once more.

And Mademoiselle left. She did not understand the whole truth. Hubert thought that perhaps they did not use it so much in France. And she could not be convinced that they had not been trying to burn her up in her chemise. They saw her off at the porte-cochère steps with as much sorrow as they could get into faces that were wanting to smile from ear to ear. They stood on the steps with their mouths and eyes drooping. Hubert felt almost as if his ears were drooping, too, like a St. Bernard. But when the democrat wagon left the grass circle and they had waved for the last time, they turned and ran. It took them half an hour of running and jumping to say farewell to Mademoiselle. Hubert decided in the first wild moments to write to Theodore.

"He ought to be told, Jane," he panted. "He'd be glad to know about it."

But of course he did not do it. Hubert never wrote letters on account of having to spell. And the dictionary was no help to him either because, as he said, if you did not know how to begin, where would you look? But somebody told Theodore, because Jane got a letter back. It said:

Dear Bite 'em, Chew 'em, and Spoo 'em Out:

A reliable informant informs me that you and Mooseer OO Bear have got rid of your ball and chain. If you want to know what I think, you've made a mistake. She might have made something of both of you. Instead of trying to set the house on fire, why not learn a thing or two?

Your loving (I don't think) brother,
Theodore B. Cares.

It was awfully hard to agree with Ted about anything, Jane felt, when she got this, but perhaps—well, anyway she was not going to tell Hubert, so she tore the letter up at once and buried it in the dog yard.

CHAPTER THREE

Grandfather's City House

It almost looked for a while as if Jane had been pushed
from the frying pan into the fire by Hubert's getting rid of
Mademoiselle. Father did not give up his idea of getting
her educated. Far from it. All the lovely month of October it must have smoldered until, as Hubert said, it had
grown from one measly governess into three whole schools.
They had been called into Father's office just before the first
of November and told about them. Edie was to go to Miss
Lincoln's. And Edie, somehow a changed character, had
nodded meekly.

"She really likes it; it isn't goodness," said Hubert as they
straggled down the hall afterwards. "She's different from
us in every way."

But he could not deny that he was pleased himself at
what was going to happen to him. There was a new boys'
school in Canboro, and Father thought Hubert might as
well try it out. Hubert firmly believed that it was better to
have a hard time with fifty boys than with one governess.
And besides, he could get there on his bicycle, or, when the
weather was bad, be driven by Pat—not a bad prospect, he
had to admit.

Only Jane was to go into exile. Not able to have the governess of his choice, Father had thought up a lot of schoolteachers instead and decided to send her to Miss Mercer's in Charlottesville.

"A school for the dumb evidently," Theodore wrote Hubert as soon as the awful news could be got to him.

Jane could live, Father thought, at the top of Grandfather's house in the city.

"Will I be alone?" Jane had asked. It was bad enough to think that she would have to live where there was no light, no sun, no air, but she and Hubert knew there was a skeleton in armor in a black cupboard in a corner of the top spare room.

"No, not alone," said Father. "Your stepmother is sacrificing her maid."

"That old Francine," thought Jane.

"She won't have to go about with you, chick," her stepmother told her later, seeing her face. "I hope you will have friends who do that, but she will take care of your room and your clothes."

And sleep with her too. She had to sleep with a French maid who drank medicine that looked like red ink out of a bottle and left long black hairs on the bureau cover.

"I don't like her smell either," she confessed to Hubert.

"Well, look out you don't get to smell like that yourself," said Hubert. "Personally, I think it's grave mold."

He would have liked to imagine that Francine's bony face had risen from the dead, but Jane jeered at him for it. There were enough other things to worry about. Those black cupboards for instance. She could not get it out of her head that they would have the power to walk at night.

But when Father said a thing, you could not get out of it, and when Madam agreed with him, then it was hopeless. They were possessed, it seemed to Jane, with this one idea of making her learnèd. So that before anyone noticed what might be happening to her, Jane was living in the top room at Grandfather's city house in Charlottesville, where he stayed in winter, with the skeleton in armor, and going every day to Miss Mercer's School.

She managed to get around the skeleton in armor more easily than she had hoped by going to sit on the stairs every night, where she could see the light below, until she could hear Francine coming up the back way to bed. But she did not know how to get around Miss Mercer's School.

After breakfast as soon as Grandfather left, Jane rollerskated to Miss Mercer's. She loved to do it; rolling over the smooth asphalt, darting ahead of the cabs and horses, mounting the sidewalk at a run, crashing into trees or iron railings for excitement or to give herself a twirl; but once in school all sense of speed and power were lost. Indeed, everything was lost. Jane herself. Here were rooms and rooms and rooms full of girls shrieking. She did not know how to shriek like that or what to shriek about. She knew still less about what to do with the silence that came next. Instead of reading poetry and coloring maps like at Miss Lincoln's, she found she was supposed to look at a blackboard or a book and learn what was said there—for life, Miss Bailey, the teacher, said. How could she? She took one look and saw that it wasn't interesting enough to remember for a minute. But the thing she knew least how to get along with was recess. She had a feeling at recess as if she were in an African jungle.

Jane walked as cautiously as she knew how through this jungle. She did not speak in case it might be impolite; she ate her lunch properly at her desk and then went out and wandered as modestly as she could around the sidewalk, mingling with girls who did not look as if they had already mingled with each other. Even so, she made a bad mistake by standing too near a group. A girl had turned round and stared at her. "Get out of here," the girl said. "Are you trying to listen?" After that she kept well down the sidewalk out of reach of hearing. When school was over, she got her hat and coat before the rest and was on her roller skates and away before the groups came pouring out the door. "Phew," she thought, flying down Brand Street, "phew." She was glad enough to get out of there alive. There was only one way to get around Miss Mercer's School and that was to pay no attention to any last, least, tiny, infinitesimal, microscopic thing about it.

Jane tried this. There was a fire-engine house at the corner of James Street, hardly two blocks from Grandfather's, where she was allowed to feed the great fat horses sugar in their stalls. There was a flower shop on Charlotte Avenue that was like the spring woods. Right in the middle of winter it smelled of moss and violets. It had them too. And besides, it had paths, banks, and corners filled with flowering plants and southern sorts of trees. On dark days she went there. Grandfather's house seemed darker than she remembered. His green parlor, which had seemed like the bottom of the sea, his dining room like an autumn forest, even his study with the firelight at dusk and the little gold letter weigher on his desk, were much less interesting than she had thought. November was a sad month anyway.

It became much, much brighter when at last she was spoken to by somebody at Miss Mercer's School. An older girl, who was called Berenice by other people, walked deliberately down the block one morning to where Jane was at recess. She stood right in front of her with her hands in her coat pockets.

"You're Jane Cares, the new girl," she said. "You are, aren't you?"

"Yes," said Jane, looking back. Berenice had brown eyes and brown hair, she noticed. She stood on her heels. She looked comfortable.

"You're all alone down here, kid," said Berenice. "Do you like it? We're all wondering if you do it on purpose."

Jane wondered if she were being teased. "Not *exactly* on purpose," she said cautiously. "I don't mind it though," she added quickly.

"You ought to, kid," said Berenice. "Come on with me." She took Jane's arm and walked her up the block. She was just pulling her into a group of other girls, when the bell rang. "Meet me after school," said Berenice, letting go Jane's arm and joining the girls ahead. "Now I have to cheese it."

Suddenly, without knowing why or wherefore, Jane had

a friend! Every day she and Berenice walked down Brand
Street together after school as if they always had and always
meant to for the rest of their lives, and all the way they did
nothing but laugh. Berenice was going to be an actress,
and she thought she might as well practice on Jane, and
Jane was delighted to know the funniest actress in the
world. They wandered about at recess too, shoving each
other off the sidewalk, bumping into other girls as carelessly
as they pleased, and giggling at themselves and each other.
When, after school, they said good-by opposite Grandfather's and Berenice said: "Let us be perfectly calm" as the
traffic trundled or pounded by, Jane had to run across practically doubled up with laughter.

There was no one to tell that she had a friend. Grown-up
people knew so little about anything that they would have
thought nothing of it. Grandfather, Madam, Father, and
probably Nellie Flaherty, Mary Bright, and even Grandfather's cook supposed that just going to school was enough.
So Jane, walking round Charlottesville told herself over
and over—not aloud but by thinking—"I've got a friend."
It seemed quite marvelous.

At least it seemed marvelous until the day some weeks
later when Berenice met her in the hall before school and
said: "I can't walk down with you today, kid." Jane was
late, so she went on into class without thinking. At recess,
when Berenice did not come out, she went back again to
her solitary place at the end of the block, still without
thinking. If she waited around, Berenice would certainly
come. And she did come finally, almost at the end of recess.

"Hello," said Jane. "Where *have* you been?" She was ready to begin laughing at once.

But Berenice walked around her without the least idea of being funny. She looked Jane all over. "You're all alone down here again, kid," she said. "If you don't like it, why did you write that letter?"

Jane tucked her braids behind her ears and stopped smiling. As far as she could remember, she never wrote letters. "What letter?" she said.

Berenice stuck her head forward. "Didn't you notice," she said, "that no one spoke to you this morning?"

"No," said Jane. "Who didn't?"

"*Nobody*," said Berenice, "would speak to the kind of person who wrote a letter like that."

Jane stared at her, and Berenice stared back. Berenice did not seem to know what to say next. "Are you *sure*—" she began to say as if she had begun to be unsure herself. Then the bell rang. "You better meet me after school, kid," she said. "*Right here.*"

Later, Jane was waiting with her skates in her hand on the edge of the sidewalk, on her toes. She was not anxious, but she felt she better be ready. She listened carefully while Berenice told her she had written a letter to Helen Proctor about Arabella Blake—a terrible letter, saying terrible things. "I wouldn't repeat them," said Berenice.

Jane did not care if she did or not. She only wanted to find out whether it was she or somebody else who was crazy. She did not know Arabella Blake, and though Helen Proctor was her desk mate, she had never really noticed her.

She told Berenice so. Still, Berenice's face did not change much.

"All right," said Jane finally. "I can prove it. Let's find Helen Proctor."

"She went home at recess. She had a headache."

"Let's go there," said Jane.

"You mean," said Berenice, peering at her, "that you would go to her house?" Jane said, yes, she would.

As they walked seriously beside each other, Jane tried to remember writing a letter to somebody. She hadn't, not even Theodore or Hubert. Or Madam. But Berenice was so sure, she wondered, alarmed, if she could have done it in her sleep. She couldn't have posted it in her sleep, though. And anyway, she had never thought about Arabella Blake at all or Helen Proctor either.

Helen did not open the door at her house, but they asked for her through the maid, and they looked up at her as she sidled along the banister.

"I didn't write you a letter about anybody," said Jane at once.

"No, not you, your mother," said Helen, fingering her glasses.

"My mother's dead," said Jane. And wishing to be as helpful as she could, she added: "You must mean my stepmother."

"Yes, that's it," said Helen quickly. "Your stepmother."

"Wrote *you* a letter?" asked Jane. "Let's see it."

"Wrote my mother a letter," said Helen, quick as lightning.

"*My* stepmother wrote your mother a letter about Arabella Blake?" said Jane slowly. *Every*body was going crazy. She turned to Berenice. "It couldn't possibly be like that," she said. "My stepmother never heard of any of you."

"Of course I couldn't let you see my mother's letter," said Helen indignantly.

"I'd like to see your mother," said Jane boldly. It seemed a fresh thing to ask to do, but Helen would not come down the stairs, and there seemed no way to get past her.

Helen's mother was resting and could not be disturbed. Helen said she hadn't been well. Jane knew she must not be fresh enough to ask to see a sick person.

"My stepmother wouldn't do it," was all she could think of to say to Berenice, but her voice wondered how she could get them to believe her.

"Well, someone did," said Helen, getting bold too. "Some one of your relations."

Berenice had to go away not quite satisfied. Jane could see it and tell it. Jane had said she could prove something, and she hadn't been able to do it.

"My stepmother lives in the country," she had to say apologetically, on the sidewalk. "I'll ask her as soon as I go home."

"I think you ought to," said Berenice.

After that Jane buckled on her skates as fast as she could.

"I might walk home with you, kid," said Berenice uncertainly as she watched her.

"Oh, no!" said Jane quickly. "Thanks a lot. I guess I'll go this way today. I'm in a hurry."

Her hurry took her right to the park. She paused only long enough at Grandfather's to sling her skates in the downstairs closet and leave her schoolbooks on the hall table. She felt that if she stopped long enough to look around and see that she was alone again, it might make her feel sick. She kept ahead of the sickness, but she could not quite keep ahead of a wild and silly wish. She wished she were some sort of princess and had some sort of prince to help her. She would not mean for this prince to stab Helen Proctor to the heart, but he might hit her on the head with the flat of a sword. And maybe he might give Berenice a slight tap too because she was so unbelieving. At any rate he would be somebody on her side. Who else was there? As she marked out her hopscotch court on a sandy path in the gardens and looked for a good flat stone, the wish came more wildly still. I wish I had somebody for Me. Why couldn't I for once— Then someone spoke to her behind her back and she jumped. A man's voice said: "Will you play? We're one short. How about joining us?"

When she looked up, there was Mr. Harris, the tutor who had lived with the Grants last year. He took a class of boys out for the afternoons and taught them games. She knew him because last summer he had lived with the Cares for a while. Theodore had had to have extra lessons before he went to boarding school, and Mr. Harris had stayed at the Red House and given them to him. Jane looked at him puzzled.

"What?" she said. She wondered if he had made a mistake and forgotten she was a girl.

"Come on," he said smiling. "It's good fun."

The rest of the afternoon was all right. Jane knew what she was doing. She knew just what to do. She flew over the ground with other flying people. Inside she thought about the Grants' tutor. He was nicer than anyone she had ever known, and he had deliberately come and chosen her. Jane looked at him constantly. He was nicer looking too! He looked like the picture of St. George in the stained-glass window of the Summerton church.

A few days after this Jane woke up one morning and found there was a lot of snow all over Charlottesville. She had known it was coming. Looking out of Grandfather's study window the night before, she had seen that Brand Street was turning to a strip of black satin. The cabs were black satin trundling over it, and the horses were satin brown, white, and black. Everything else was getting white, as if it had been shaken over by a sugar sifter, and before she went to bed flakes had begun to come down fast and thick, hushing all sounds, and turning the street lamps to fat yellow stars. In the morning she was waked by a hollow grating noise beyond the window. It was the "outside men" with wooden shovels clearing sidewalks. It was a wonderful noise, but she could hardly bear to have them do it, wasting so much good snow. But she knew the park gardens could not be scraped, and there was a hill, two hills, there for coasting.

That afternoon she could not wait to get to the park. Mr. Harris and the boys would certainly be there, and she could certainly coast with them. She picked up her sled in

Grandfather's cellar and dragged it impatiently over the scraped bricks. But at the bottom of the first park hill she looked things over blankly. It was a mass of babies on their high red sleds and in their elegant pink coats being chased by nurses and told to hold on tight. What a sight! Mr. Harris and the boys must have gone to the north hill. It was farther away, straight across the gardens and then at the other end of the park, but it was better and higher. Usually it was used solely by the North-Enders who came up from the other side of Charlottesville and acted as if they owned that part of it. But Jane thought that today everyone could have a turn at the north hill.

Her confidence was a little shaken as she left the smaller shelter of the gardens. The park swept up a long open slope unbroken by a tree or bench or path except the middle one that she was on. She did not like to be so much in sight. She searched for the Grants' tutor hopefully, or any familiar face. *Was* she meant to be here?

At the top of the hill Jane knew right away she was in the wrong place. The crowd of yelling boys did not seem to see her. They put their elbows, shoulders, and feet where she was standing without looking whether she was there or not. She stood with her sled held against her chest ready to take her turn, but boy after boy shoved past her and went flying down the hill, howling. Hurriedly she looked for another girl and realized for the first time that she was the only girl there. Where the sense of danger came from she had no idea, but suddenly she had it. She wanted to crouch as if she were a rabbit. The least move, the slightest

action, would attract attention, and she must get away
from there before they really saw her. Slowly and carefully
she turned away from the face of the hill and walked a
few steps before putting down her sled. Her neck and the
backs of her legs felt as if they had been peeled. But she
heard no sounds from the boys except their shouting, and
with a quick run she flung herself forward and coasted to
the park's central path. "Safe," she thought. "I'm lucky."
She would get away to the more familiar gardens, *quick*.

As she picked up the rope of her sled, relieved all
through, she had to watch another sled draw up beside her
own. She had been relieved too soon. One of the boys had
followed her. She did not want to raise her eyes to look at
him, but her head had to come up. The boy was one of
those town-toughs. He was an awful tough with hair that
grew right out of his eyebrows, and green teeth. She could
see them all because he was grinning at her as if she was
supposed to like it.

Jane had had lots of experience with country toughs.
At least once a winter they came up the Summerton main
street in a gang, and there was a snowball fight either going to or coming from Miss Lincoln's. Occasionally the
toughs and the Cares had fought with rotten apples, and
once Theodore had arranged an ambush, with some other
boys from the west end to help him, and the toughs had
been chased back across the railroad tracks in a terrible
defeat. Jane had helped with that. But this was not one of
the Summerton kind, who most of the time were just a lot
of boys who lived around town. This one had green teeth.

Jane had to tell herself to go on living and moving quietly. Once in a while she heard her sled making a shirring noise on the dry asphalt where the path had been cleared, but most of the time her usual senses seemed to have deserted her, and a new one told her without seeing or without hearing that the tough was following her all the way.

Although she reached Grandfather's perfectly well, from this day on for many days, when she was outdoors, Jane had to keep her eyes on the ground and was forced to know through her new sense that somewhere in the offing was the tough. As if he had nothing else in the world to do, he came every morning and escorted her to school and came back in the afternoon and escorted her home. He kept his distance, staying on the opposite sidewalk, and he could not keep up with her roller skates, but he was there all the time. The shame and disgrace of it! To have someone following you up and down Brand Street, following you all day everywhere. She would not go to the gardens to meet Mr. Harris and the boys with such an escort. If she went to Charlotte Avenue to look in shop windows, he might not be there at first, but he came, he came and stood around looking at her. He even waited opposite Grandfather's for her to come out. Or he seemed to. She could not see him from the window, but as soon as she was on the street he was there too. In her distraction she wondered whether, because she had been ass enough almost to pray for a protector, she had been sent this thing. Finally she would not go outdoors any more. Nellie Flaherty told her what happened to the health of girls who stayed indoors continually, Mary Bright told her about consumption, the cook said cookies were not for those who would never take a breath of air, but Jane sat in front of Grandmother's old dollhouse and pretended afternoon after afternoon that she loved it.

She could do this until Hubert was sent in to stay with her for Saturday and Sunday, and even then she embarked on a forlorn hope of interesting him in something in the house. But Hubert had glimpsed a better world. He had seen in the morning paper which Grandfather had foolishly left on the floor by the dining-room table, that there was a Sportsman's Show in town, and he was going to go. Jane had better come with him because, if she didn't, he would know for sure that she only liked dolls.

"All right," said Jane. "But I use the back door now."

"Why?"

"It's more exciting."

"If you like garbage," said Hubert, but he shrugged his shoulders.

Going out the back door had been a good idea, and there was such a crowd in the enormous World Building that they were satisfactorily lost. But they made the mistake of stopping to buy popcorn, and then Hubert seemed to have known something all along.

"Jane," he said, "there's a funny-looking guy goes everywhere that we go; see him?"

"No!" said Jane.

Hubert strolled to another booth to look at some more

guns. Jane tried to push him along faster. That made Hubert suspicious.

"Is that guy following *you?*"

"No!" said Jane.

She shut her lips and kept her eyes straight ahead until they were behind the door at Grandfather's again. Hubert went at once to look out the window.

"Christmas cats!" he said. "The guy's still there! Have you got a follower, Jane?"

"If you say such a thing as that," said Jane, taking a stride toward the fireplace, "I'll beat you with the andirons." She grabbed one and stood there. Hubert considered her. Although he often thought that now he could beat Jane up, she was still just a little bigger than he was.

"For heaven's sake," he said, sitting down in Grandfather's chair and splaying out his legs. "I was only wondering how such a thing could possibly be. Do you want to get rid of him?" he added.

"Yes!" said Jane.

"Well, I wouldn't know how," said Hubert, looking at his boots, "and that's a fact."

That night, however, without Jane's knowing it, he decided to ask Theodore's advice. While she was concentrating on some sort of schoolbook, he wrote Theodore a letter. "Jane has a follower," he said. "Anyway she has a guy who follows her. All over town. She doesn't like him. Neither do I. His teeth are green. Can you devise any way to get rid of this guy?" He went out himself very quietly and put the letter in the post box on the corner.

The next day was Sunday, and Jane's follower was not there when they came out with Grandfather to walk to church. The rest of the day Jane absolutely commanded Hubert to stay in the house.

"But he's gone!" said Hubert.

"He comes back," said Jane.

After lunch Hubert, investigating from the dollhouse room window, found this was true. Just the same he was desperate. There was skating in the park, and he wasn't going to play with a dollhouse all day. She ought to know that. He volunteered to go out in the street and meet the tough.

"What good will that do?" asked Jane.

"I could say you're too young for him. Maybe he'd vamoose."

He did actually go out and he crossed the street. Jane watched from the window. The tough grinned with all his teeth showing, took a swipe at Hubert in a fooling way, which Hubert leaned back to avoid, and went to lean on the area railings of the opposite house while he picked his green teeth. Hubert came back.

"He won't go," he said.

Grandfather made Jane take Hubert to the train. Nellie Flaherty had probably talked to him about health and air and consumption. Jane thought it would have been much wiser if they had worried about her heart stopping on account of having to come home when it was nearly dark with her follower behind her. She held onto the bell until Nellie opened the door.

"No need to tear the house down, Miss," said Nellie.

There was need, there was great need, only some people were stupid enough not to know it. Jane went upstairs and surreptitiously pulled down all the shades in the front of the house while Nellie was lighting the lamps behind her. She didn't know what good it did, but she *had* to do it.

When she went home for the next week-end, Madam was not there. She and Father had gone to Florida, Nurse said, and would be back sometime. So she could not ask about Helen Proctor's letter. Anyway she forgot about it. She tried to forget everything about the city of Charlottesville, where the tough was, and, besides, Hubert was teasing her to look at a letter of his. It was from Ted in answer to one he had written about her predicament.

"I won't read it," said Jane. "You're a traitor for telling him."

"Just look at one line," said Hubert. "It might be valuable."

Jane looked at the folded part of the letter he held out.

"Tell her to hit him in the snoot," it said.

In all her eleven years she had never known Theodore to give advice that did the least good.

Jane was so used to keeping her head down and her eyes on the pavement on the way to school, and indeed, to be on the safe side, up the steps and in the door, that she did not see Berenice waiting for her the next morning. Her mind too was on other things. Her follower had been just a block away.

She only thought it a little queer that Miss Bailey looked

up and nodded to her—extra. What had happened to *her,* Jane wondered. She would not nod and smile when she knew Jane hadn't done one single piece of homework. She had been too busy forgetting things and managing Chris on the snowy roads, and at night she had toppled over on her books and gone to sleep. She was even more surprised and still indifferent when the first thing Miss Bailey said was: "Jane Cares, the headmistress wishes to see you."

With everyone in the room smiling with glee, Miss Mercer must be going to give her the dickens for something, Jane thought. Then, suddenly, her heart contracted so it almost pinched her. Miss Mercer wanted to see her because she had seen the follower. They were grinning because they all knew it. On her way to the headmistress's office she had only a minute to think what to do. She couldn't kill Miss Mercer—she had no gun—but she could say nothing, nothing, nothing at all. She would not even open her mouth to say "good morning" for fear something else might come out.

"Jane," said Miss Mercer, tapping a pencil against her desk.

Jane nodded.

"Helen Proctor has been to see me this morning. She told me what I have been expecting to hear. The story about the letter was a pure invention." Miss Mercer stopped. Jane, though she was looking hard at the headmistress, had not quite been able to shift her mind. "Are you listening?" asked Miss Mercer.

Jane nodded again, trying to remember what had just

been said. If it was what she thought, she had never heard anything so absolutely unimportant in the whole of her life. Well, she was glad Madam hadn't written any foolish letters, but she had known this all the time. She sat on the edge of the chair and tried to look interested because Miss Mercer was talking again.

"Helen will apologize to you before the whole class."

"Oh, no!" said Jane before she meant to.

Miss Mercer gave her a long steady glance with her head on one side. "And if I were you, Jane," she said, "I should pay more attention to my classmates. They may want you to."

Jane half-slid, half-ran out of the headmistress's office. No, oh no, it would be terrible to pay attention to anyone now; it would be awful to have them speaking to her, staying around. They would finally be sure to see the tough cross the street!

After school it was just as she expected and worse. Nobody mentioned Helen Proctor or the apology she had grinningly made, but Jane might as well have been caught on sticky flypaper as get away from the girls who were trying to walk down the hall with her to the coat closet. Berenice pushed through them. She said she meant to go with her. Jane struggled politely to get out of it. She made all the excuses she could think of quickly. She said she always skated now. That she wasn't going down Brand Street. Berenice only took her arm and pulled her out the door.

"You're coming, kid," she said. "I need to apologize to you myself."

And then, although she did not really look, Jane knew that today, this time, the follower was not there. It was a miracle! Really a miracle after those days and days and at this exact time. She looked up and down; she looked almost into the sky. No, he was *not* there. She felt like air. She and Berenice laughed and laughed all the way down Brand Street just as if nothing had ever happened, just as if she had a friend again. When they reached Grandfather's, Jane did not go in. It was too much fun; it was too good a day to go in even for a minute. She would go straight to the park and find Mr. Harris and the boys. She had never felt so well able to do anything at all. She almost had to laugh too hard. Once Berenice shook her.

"Don't be such a silly kid," she said. "You'll give yourself hysterics."

Jane became quiet at once until Berenice pushed her off the sidewalk again. They had a wonderful time. And this kept up even after Berenice had had to go straight on to her own house and Jane turned off to the gardens. Mr. Harris was there with a new set of boys. They were a little younger than the others, and Jane was put in charge of two of them. Would she mind, Mr. Harris asked, showing them how to run a relay. She said she wouldn't, but she was glad nature had fixed it so that you couldn't just fly to pieces when you felt fine. She needed all of herself together to try to do what Mr. Harris wanted.

She tried to do this so enthusiastically that she forgot that nature liked you to look where you were going. Turning back to encourage her pupils, after she had run on ahead of them, she came too near the wooden walk that covered the garden paths in winter. Jane did not even know her ankle had turned over. She felt her foot slip down from the wood to dirt, and knew she had tripped and gone down; the boys had to jump over her. The next thing was that she was sitting up on the sandy path with the fiercest pain she had ever had. It was so fierce it seemed to twist her face in all directions, and although she did not want to, she had to rock backwards and forwards and swing herself from side to side. The boys got scared and ran off to the other end of the gardens to get Mr. Harris. Jane managed to get up and hop to the bench where she had left her books. By the time they all got back she was sure she would be all right. But now she closed her eyes a minute waiting for the pain to lessen. Much too soon there was a thump on the bench beside her. She tried quickly to straighten out her face; she let her ankle go and looked up brightly. She was not going to have to give up all the fun just because of a silly twisted ankle. It would be all right in just a minute. Jane was opening her mouth to tell Mr. Harris so as she turned her head.

There on the bench beside her, just the other side of her geography book, was the tough. He wasn't looking at her; he was looking straight out across the gardens, but he was smiling, a wide green smile. Jane was so shocked she might have screamed without being able to help it if her anger had not come so quickly. It leaped through her as if it had been pumped boiling hot from her feet. This was not fair. This was the last thing. The Grants' tutor would be coming in a minute. Berenice would be walking home with her again tomorrow. They would think this was hers! In a flash came Theodore's advice. In a flash Jane had hold of her heavy geography book. The tough sat there grinning, and she raised the book and hit him. When he turned toward her, she hit him again; she hit him on the snoot, hard, and it began to bleed. Finally her outrage and anger growing to an explosion, she slammed the book against his upraised hands. "There!" she whispered furiously, "leave me alone!" Then she saw blood coming through the tough's fingers, and the Grants' tutor in the distance, and she ran. As far as she knew, her ankle was as good as new. She felt no pain at all. She used it to fly. She skimmed out the gate, across Hartford Street. She dodged cabs and she dodged the policeman; voices called after her, Mr. Harris' voice shouted from the gate; she simply put on more speed. She didn't know *what* she was running for, but she was sure, she was dead sure, they would all be after her, and she had better get to Grandfather's and hide. She was, presently, safely inside his double doors, from where she peered down the street. It was empty and quiet. She tried to get her breath before she rang the bell, but something more was happening to her that she wasn't expecting. A red hot iron was being run through her ankle and being turned round and round. After she had rung the bell, she sat down in the cold marble entrance. When

Mary Bright opened the door, she was holding her leg and rocking back and forth. Mary Bright looked at her as if she were a display of fireworks, with her mouth open.

"I guess you better get the doctor," gasped Jane. "I guess I've hurt myself."

It was quite a few days before she was able to walk. In the meantime it was not bad fun, she thought, in the third-floor room in the daytime. She was able to send Francine on errands just as she liked. She sent her for gum, and books, and peppermints, and on Sunday she made her bring the "funny papers" on the way back from church. Grandfather puffed up to see her once a day and brought fruit in his pockets. Cook waddled up with cookies and desserts and asked what she would like to eat. Jane ordered sweetbreads, artichokes, steak, and ice cream as many times as she could. She ate nearly half a chocolate soufflé herself. Her ankle hurt all the time, but not nearly so much when people were doing whatever she asked them to. But there was one thing the matter. The skeleton in armor. Now that she was tied down, he and the other black cupboards crept toward her at night. The only way she could keep them all at a distance was to stare from one to the other unceasingly, so that it was important to stay awake until Francine came up from the kitchen. On Francine's night out Jane had to work hard and late. But as hard as she worked, she fell asleep watching and had a nightmare. It took all day to get over the night, and by that time it was there again. Jane didn't know what to do. She really didn't know. It was as bad as having a follower. She had got rid of the daytime one, but now he was on her trail at night.

It was quite a few days before Father and Madam came to see her because they had to get back from Florida. Jane did not expect them because Grandfather had sent a telegram to say that all she had done was sprain her ankle. And she was not quite sure she *wanted* to see them. Two people had called on Grandfather. Nellie Flaherty said so. One was Miss Mercer—she knew that—and one was the Grants' tutor. By the time Father and Madam came to see her, it was very likely that they would know that educating her was a hard job and that she had broken a tough's nose. About the first, she would have disappointed Madam, and about the second she had heard of a thing called "assault and battery." Did you get put in jail for it? She didn't know if they could save her. She wondered sometimes if she could get them to want to save her.

When Father and Madam did get home and came to Grandfather's, it was almost the middle of the night. Jane had gone to sleep after a long fight with the cupboards, and when some people insisted that she wake up, she was cross.

"No," she said. "I don't want to."

When someone spoke to her a second time, she moved her shoulder out of reach.

"Go away," she said fretfully. "It's too late now."

Father moved away to the end of the bed, but Madam kept on standing near her. "It's after eleven o'clock," said Jane, explaining, when she realized who was there.

"It is late, Janey," her stepmother said, smiling down at

her, "but you'd better wake up, chick, and hear what I say. We're taking you home for a little while."

Jane opened her eyes. "Now?" she said.

"In the morning."

Jane thought she had better not pose as a wounded hero. Had they or hadn't they talked to Grandfather?

"What about all the other things?" she asked, trying to hold onto her breath.

"They're settled," said Madam.

Jane searched her eyes. They were all right. She didn't have to look at Father. He would have to be all right too. A whole river full of words seemed to rush up through her to give to her stepmother.

"I simply couldn't do the Latin," she said. "I suppose I got fired. What shall I have to do now?"

"How would you like," Madam said, "to be helped by the Grants' tutor when you come back to Charlottesville?"

CHAPTER FOUR

Father's Friend

Theodore and Jane came home for the Christmas vacation, both of them on the same train from Charlottesville, and Hubert and Edie met them at the station. Not that they were pining to see them, Hubert explained—it had been fairly peaceful at home for a while—but he had some news. Edie just went for the ride. There had been snow, not a lot, but enough so that Pat was going to use the big sleigh. It would be good fun, Hubert agreed, to sit in the back seat covered by the buffalo robe and be a Lord and Lady out for an airing. They started away from the porte-cochère looking about them grandly as Pat coaxed May and June, the stout little cobs, to skim them along. But halfway there, Hubert had got tired of so much distinction, and going up the village hill, he had peered over the back of the seat. He just did it, he said, to see if there might be a wolf on their track.

"We could throw him the rug first," he had said. "He could worry that for a while." He did not say what would happen after that. But Edie would not go on being a lady out for an airing. She got under the rug and stayed there, even after the sleigh reached the station. So Hubert enjoyed the luck he had made for himself and used it by standing, without responsibilities, as near the edge of the station platform as possible so that he could be nearly run down and chopped into bits by the roaring engine wheels. After that he went to stare at the cowcatcher and think of its tossing off cows, until Jane and Theodore came up and pushed him with their suitcases.

"Oh," he said. "I thought you hadn't come yet."

They were there all right, they assured him, and they had even seen Mr. Haynes, the stationmaster, about their trunks, so would he please wake up because they wanted to get home and take off their awful city clothes.

"Well, don't sit on Edie," said Hubert. "She's under the rug on account of wolves."

They moved her carefully onto the floor and rested their feet on her.

"Well, what's up?" Theodore asked, after they had had time to notice who was going by on the main street, how much snow there was on the stone walls, and whether the trees and houses were exactly as they had left them.

"Oh, yes!" said Hubert, rather shocked at himself. "I nearly forgot. Do you know what's happened at home? Father has a friend."

"I didn't know he had any," said Theodore.

"Where?" asked Jane.

"Right at the house. He came one day and he's staying."

Hubert, himself, had discovered him. He had come in one day from school and found a man walking up and down the front hall. He had kept his eye on him from the

dining room while he had cake and milk. But when the
man asked for some too, Hubert thought he must be all
right, and they had had a conversation. His name was Mr.
Carpenter, and whether Theodore and Jane would believe
it or not, he had a beard. "It's red," said Hubert.

"Well?" said Theodore.

"I don't see where he'll sleep," said Jane. All the rooms
in the Red House that she could see in her mind had someone in them.

Mr. Carpenter, Hubert said, was living in a tent in the
backyard. What did they think of that? He was an explorer
and had nearly been to the North Pole.

"What's he exploring now?" Theodore asked. "The bees
and the rabbits?"

"Don't be so funny," said Hubert. "I haven't told you
anything yet. He crossed the Atlantic Ocean in a sailboat
with a cat. The cat got drowned, but Mr. Carpenter didn't.
That's exploring, isn't it? I'd like to see you do it."

"And I'll tell you one more thing," said Hubert, as Pat
clucked to the cobs as they reached the bottom of the village hill. "We're going on an expedition ourselves after
Christmas."

"In a sailboat, I suppose," said Theodore negligently.

Edie suddenly stuck her head out of the buffalo rug.
"Then I won't go," she said. "I don't like the old things.
Jane," she added hoarsely, "I'll tell you something. He
tipped that boat over."

"She doesn't know what she's talking about," said
Hubert, as they turned into the yard. "And if you don't

stop," he added fiercely, "I'll step on your face." Mr. Carpenter's boat, he explained hurriedly, had been shipwrecked. It was not a good boat anyhow.

Hubert was not nearly satisfied by the time they were all getting out under the porte-cochère. But he could not get Theodore or Jane to pay any more attention. They were home. First they had to change into their Summerton skins. Then maybe they would see. To tell the truth there were so many things to do when they first got home it was hard to know— Their stepmother was in the hall to greet them. Jane got a kiss. "Not a peck, a real kiss, pressed in, for love you know," Madam said, smiling. She knew exactly how to do it. She shook hands with Ted as if she meant the same thing, and then let them go. On the way upstairs Jane decided what would be next. As soon as she saw Theodore going out through the backyard to saddle Cinder, she made her escape the back way too. She went all over the home lot running her hands against everything —heavens, no, not Mr. Carpenter's tent, which she saw suddenly in front of her—but, making a wide swerve, Aunt Charlotte's wall, not minding if she scratched her hand on the rosebush, the carriage house, the watering trough. After pulling up the sleeves of her jacket, she put both arms into the water above the elbow and let them stay there, freezing. No matter where she went or what she did, it did not seem to be enough. Beyond the pony paddock she picked up handfuls of snow and smeared it over her face and arms. In the blue and orange twilight she plodded the entire circuit of the Big Field and after that felt so much better that she could go in and eat the last piece of cake that they had left for tea.

Theodore and Jane met Hubert's Mr. Carpenter when they came down to the library before dinner. Although he had on two sweaters instead of a coat, and a pair of bed-room slippers, he shook hands with them with great polite-ness. Then he went and stood as far as he could from the library fire, looking out the window at the snow with his hands behind his back.

"Johnny Cares," he said, "your house is overheated."

Nobody answered him. Madam smiled, but Father just stood a little more in the center of the fireplace.

At dinner they discussed the "expedition." It was to be to a place in the North where Mr. Carpenter had a small house. He also had a new kind of automobile that would go anywhere and do anything. He wanted Father to give up the terrible way he was living and get out on the road for a bit. He wanted him to harden up and not get old.

Nobody could eat properly because they were so inter-ested in Father getting a lecture.

Mr. Carpenter showed him what was the matter—cigar-smoking, whiskey-drinking, having Pat meet him at the station with the democrat. He saw, he said, that Father was "putting on flesh."

Neither Father nor Madam seemed to hear him, and Father drank his highball and lit his cigar right in Mr. Carpenter's face. Just the same it began to seem as if the expedition were going to take place. The wonderful car was in the carriage house at that moment.

They were not to be allowed, however, to go to the Far North unless they were "in condition." Father *had* heard all Mr. Carpenter had been saying and agreed with it. Cold baths in the mornings, and no "slops" like root beer —or bulls' eyes or licorice sticks. On account of Christmas there was no money left over for "slops," and the bathroom was so flooded for several mornings that Nurse said they were on their way to their deaths, but the enthusiasm for being in condition stopped when Father and Madam and Mr. Carpenter went to Charlottesville on a pre-Christmas visit to Grandfather. There did not seem to be any more time for it, because as the days of the vacation went on, there was more and more snow of the best kind. God, Theodore felt one morning when the sun was blazing, was certainly on their side.

"If it isn't just the weather man," said Edie, who was licking snowballs when she could find one without any wool from somebody's mittens.

The others thought she was being sacrilegious.

"Do you want to be turned into a pillow of salt?" asked Hubert severely. "You'd be washed away in the first rain, you know."

He and Jane were grateful for such a wonderful day for punging, their favorite sport of hitching their sleds behind sleighs, and he was not going to let Edie tempt God to spoil it. In fact, they were just hanging round by their fort wondering what was going to become of her for the rest of the day. Two was company, but three was certainly a crowd, punging. She saved them herself. She was going to track rabbits, she said. She did this with Fatty McHenry, using him for a hound, and Jane and Hubert watched her cross the road and get under the McHenrys' black iron fence with great pleasure. They watched Theodore go off across the Big Field—only falling three times—on skis. Then they ran for their sleds.

In all their lives, Jane and Hubert agreed, red-faced and almost frozen as they rose from their sleds way out on the outskirts of Canboro, they had never had such punging. It was not only the snow—but of course it *was* the snow, Jane pointed out—but sleighs and sleds had gone past every few minutes all morning. All they had had to do was stand behind the chestnut tree at the end of the circular drive and just as a sleigh went by dash out and as quietly as possible hook their ropes to the runners. The last one had been Milldale Smith who had three extra lashes to his whip especially for pungers, but it was always worth risking because his horse was so fast. They had managed to get nearly to Canboro with him and to slip their ropes just before he turned into a drive. It was a terrific triumph. It had been all the better because Hubert had nearly been brained by one of the horse's snowballs that had come bouncing under the sleigh. He now knew what it was like to go to war and have cannon balls go whizzing past.

A few nights later Jane came out of her room ready for dinner and met the boys at the top of the stairs.

"Did you know there was a moon?" she said.

They did know.

"Coasting on the Main Dairy hill," said Theodore simply. "Eat fast, kids, we'll take the double-runner."

They did eat fast and almost spoiled the evening. Father noticed Hubert putting in a piece of corn-bread whole. But Hubert managed to come up to the scratch. He stretched his cheeks like a squirrel and chewed on and on, washing it down with milk and looking innocently back at Father.

"I thought my mouth was bigger," he said meekly.

They ate their dessert in dainty sips after that, but when they reached the foot of the stairs later, they dashed.

"Tally-ho," said Theodore under his breath.

The Main Dairy hill was a giant. The road started in a little wood, went steeply round a corner, dashed past lights and buildings, and then ran just at good coasting strength down between the meadows into full quiet moonlight.

"This is training for you," Theodore said exultantly as they trailed up it for the twentieth time.

Just as the moon was at its very best and was going to change and get later and smaller, it had a golden ring. The boys groaned at it, and Theodore spit through his teeth and said some swear words, but they could not change the golden ring, and it did what it meant to do. They all hoped and prayed it would be a blizzard, but it was not. It was warm weather and rain. The Cares had to watch the snow vanishing as if it were a jerked-off blanket, and then they had to watch Summerton and all the meadows being soaked with water they could do nothing with and little

shining shallow ponds that were perfectly useless. Hubert
fixed himself a place in his bathtub to read, Theodore
cleaned the guns in the gun cupboard, and Jane tried to
teach Edie to play parcheesi. They were sorry, but if Father
couldn't do anything about the weather, training had to
stop.

Just then, while the whole of Summerton was still covered with pools and ponds and the Reservoir was clear and
brown, there came a cold snap. Everything was made to
freeze up by one still mighty breath, even the boys' radia-
tor, which they had shut off under an open window, thinking that getting accustomed to lots of fresh air would be
useful at the Far North.

It was not at all useful when the water leaked through
the ceiling into Father's breakfast. Theodore tried to stop
the fountain by stuffing the hole with his pajama suit, but
Hubert gave up and sat on an island of sheets and blankets, waiting, he said, for a boat. He did not say this to
Father, though. He said it to Gander who flew downstairs
like a hen, making the same kind of noise. The boys had to
spend the day handing the plumber his tools and pledge a
month's allowance to pay for the damage, but the morning
after this Pat told Cook when he came in for breakfast and
Cook told Gander and Gander told Father that there was
skating on the Reservoir.

"Can we go, sir?" asked Theodore politely.

Father looked at him and at the ceiling and at Hubert
and Jane and Edie, "I suppose you would go anyhow," he

said. "But I think," he added, turning the pages of his paper with a wide sweep, "this time I shall have to ask you to take Harry."

Mr. Carpenter was much pleased to come and train them on the Reservoir ice. Although he had wooden skates that tied on, kept his arms clasped behind his back, and wore a red knitted cap with a tassel, they had to admit that he could skate. Theodore, puffing and blowing, could not even tie him. He had probably learned on the polar ice, Hubert thought, and after he had had this idea wondered why no one ever skated to the North Pole. Jane knew better than that.

"It's in cakes like you put in the ice chest, goat," she said.

Hubert was sorry to hear it. He had been thinking of doing exploring when he grew up.

At night Mr. Carpenter built a fire for them on a little part of the McHenrys' lawn, and Madam came over from the Red House and skated herself like a picture of a ship on a calm ocean.

Christmas Day itself, however, in spite of the cold snap, was what Theodore called "a doubtful feast." The doubtfulness began the day before when they were found in a cluster at the front door just starting off for the drugstore with twenty-five cents that Hubert had found jiggling round in the lining of his knickerbockers. Unfortunately Father had been interested in where they were going. "Slops again," he said. "Do you know where *I* am going?" he asked. He had given them the gimlet eye, Hubert remembered. "To feed the poor," he had added. And he wanted them to think about it. They did all the way to the drugstore, and it cast a gloom over the afternoon.

"Gee," said Hubert, "if I thought about the poor, I'd have to begin with myself." He pulled out his pockets and wore them that way to show what he meant. But it did not cheer them up, and Father did not take the hint. He shook his head at Madam during dinner as he carefully tipped off the ash of his cigar and told her that youth was deteriorating.

This seemed to affect the Christmas presents the next morning. No one was quite sure they got what they wanted except Edie. Edie was given, by Mr. Carpenter, a small brown hairy dog. It jumped out of its box and into her arms, and she knew at once that its name was Widgy. No one could get her to see that it might be anything else.

In spite of the usual family dinner at Uncle Charles's, where Big Nora caught her frizzled pompadour on fire with the plum pudding and had to be put out, Mr. Carpenter's expedition became more and more important. The principal thing about it was that it made Father cheer up.

"It's the thought of us being put to the greasy grind," Theodore said, dropping nuts into his mouth that he had saved from Uncle Charles's dinner. They had come upstairs and were sitting round the hall-table lamp in the alcove outside the nursery after having been told in the library what to expect in the Far North. Father and Mr. Carpenter had wanted to be sure they understood. No luxuries. A very simple existence.

"How simple?" Hubert had asked.

"You will have the unique opportunity, Hubert, of hewing wood and drawing water," said Father, pointing his cigar directly at him.

"That means no heat and no pump," said Theodore flatly. "Take that in, Falstaff."

Standing in front of the fireplace shoulder to shoulder with Mr. Carpenter, Father gave the final edict: "We don't expect any complaints." To their surprise Edie was to be allowed to take Widgy, although there were edicts about him too. "If you can't make your soul-mate behave," Father said poetically, "out he goes on the 'reef of Norman's Woe.' "

"What did he *mean?*" asked Edie. "I never heard of that place."

"Sure death," said Theodore, "that's all. So look out." And he urged her to remember that she couldn't run to Madam for protection. Madam wasn't going. She had had too bad a cold.

There had been one other disappointment in the plans. They had been told that they were not to go in the wonderful car. There wasn't room. They were obliged to see that this was so. They had all been out to examine the auto time after time and wondered themselves how it was going to be managed. They had been told now that they were to go by train to the end of the railroad and be met by a man with a wagon. He would take them to Mr. Carpenter's small house where, "skipping up by road" as Mr. Carpenter described it, he and Father would be to meet them.

"Take all your warm clothes," said Father in a good humor at last. "And a change of everything."

There could not have been a better day to start an expedition than the one they woke up to on the right morning. It was cold, but the sun was out, and there was no wind. The road in front of the Red House looked hard and perfect, though they did not think this mattered because they had heard that Mr. Carpenter's perfect auto had perfect tires and some new perfect arrangement to put on the tires if there was any mud or snow. And there could not have been a better sight than Father and Mr. Carpenter starting off. "The two bears, as I live and breathe," said Theodore as they trooped out the front door to see them. The men had so many clothes on, they spread over the sides of the front seat, and Pat was also tucking the buffalo rug around Father's knees. But whatever they looked like, Jane thought, the car was a race horse. And it was panting to start.

Madam came out behind them and stood at the steps. Father and Mr. Carpenter lifted their goggles.

"Good-by, Elsie," Father called, "only forty-five miles. Don't worry; couldn't be easier. Don't make any mistakes, kids." Mr. Carpenter took off his cap and waved it three times round his head. The auto went out of the yard with a beautiful plume of steam coming out of the back and was off up the road and out of sight like a bird. Nobody had time to be mournful. Before Madam went back into the house, she saw them all and their suitcases and

Widgy into the democrat wagon and waved them off to the station.

The train trip pleased everybody. Father had given Ted some extra money, and he was very liberal with it. They crossed the tracks to Mr. Shrewsbury's and were allowed to buy their favorite funny papers.

"It's because he wants to read the sporting page himself," said Hubert, the disillusioned. But he felt it was unimportant as long as he had Happy Hooligan for himself.

Theodore also encouraged them to buy gum, especially Edie and Widgy. "It'll stick their jaws together for a while," he said. And it did, for quite a while. It also made Edie go up and down the train for water, which kept her exercised and busy.

Mr. Wood met them just as he was supposed to. He had a milk wagon, full of hay, on runners, which they thought much better than a sleigh. It was a surprise, though, to find snow there and such a lot of it, but it pleased them a great deal. Only Theodore frowned at it. He wondered if Father and Mr. Carpenter knew this.

"They must have *some* sense," said Jane. So they forgot all about them.

The drive in the milk sleigh was long and smooth and cold. Colder than it might have been because the sun had gone in. Theodore sat on the box and talked to Mr. Wood and every once in a while chawed off a piece of chocolate and put it in his cheek. The others lay in the straw and passed Widgy around. Settled on their stomachs, he made a good hot-water bottle. Every so often one of them peered over the side to see what was there, but as it was always the same, great white stretches of snow, they talked about where they were being taken.

"He said it was a house," said Hubert firmly because Jane was saying obstinately that they were going to a cabin.

House or cabin, they certainly expected to come to a place where the wonderful auto would be standing, a door would be opened, and voices would say, "Here they are." Therefore, after they had finally left the white open fields and slid for a while through a hemlock forest and then dipped down a wooded hill and up another and found themselves in front of an old house and some old maple trees where there was nothing and nobody, they were surprised. Jane and Hubert, kneeling at the side of the sleigh, thought it was the deadest looking house they had ever seen. Theodore himself, though he kept his jaws going professionally, seemed to be looking at it doubtfully. Nevertheless, Mr. Wood stopped his horses in front of it.

"Say," he said. "I guess yer folks ain't come yet."

That was clear to them all. But Mr. Wood was wonderfully nice to them. He collected all their suitcases in one great armful and carried them up the snowy steps to the door. Then he went back and brought up a large box.

"Yer groceries," he said.

He found the key in one of his pockets and let them in.

"Suffering cats!" said Theodore when the door was opened and they followed Mr. Wood's heels into a square sitting-room.

"It's a mite cold, ain't it, sonny," Mr. Wood said.

Jane would have liked to say that she wouldn't stay here, not for a minute, that she didn't like it, but Edie said it for her and turned toward the door.

"Wait!" said Theodore commandingly.

Edie plumped herself and Widgy down on a chair and waited.

"Yer folks are coming, sure thing?" asked Mr. Wood. He pulled a letter out of his pocket and took a look at the outside of it. "Hmmmm," he said. "Well, I'll just start the fire for ye."

He had to go out to the back for kindling because there did not seem to be any among the great pile of logs by the fireplace, and for paper he "borrowed" Hubert's Happy Hooligan. He waited on his haunches for the fire to catch and kindle. When it was going brightly, he put on one of the big logs and watched until that caught. The room did not get much warmer, but the Cares could feel that it was going to. Edie put Widgy down and let him run around and sniff.

But Mr. Wood was not comfortable. They could see that. He looked at the fire and he looked at them and he looked all round the sitting room. He did not know what to do with them next. They did not know what to do with him either. Theodore began to unwind his muffler.

"Gut to see to my cows," Mr. Wood said doubtfully.

"Sure thing," said Theodore.

It took another long minute for Mr. Wood to make up his mind, but he finally moved toward the door.

"Keep yer eye on that fire," he said, looking back, "and yer'll be all right."

As soon as they had watched his horses pull him down into the woods, they rushed for the door and looked down the road they had come. It was a beautiful road bordered with pines decked with snow, but it was empty.

"Crimping Christmas," said Theodore. "Where *are* they?"

After they had gone in again sadly and eyed the fire and come out again expectantly and gone in and come out and gone in and come out, something made them think that this was a waste of time. Theodore examined the sky. "How about a little exploring?" he said.

"I'm game," said Hubert.

"What about the fire?" asked Jane.

Edie hoped that there would not be any bears.

As soon as they were started and had left that unwelcoming house behind, they felt sure they were doing the right thing. It lasted too long, that was the only trouble with it. The loggers' road that they found leading down through the woods went too far in the first place, and when it came out at an abandoned cabin and they found a porcupine had a hole under it, it took too long to see if he was there. Jane and Hubert spent much too much time crossing and recrossing a little river in front of the cabin. Edie and Widgy followed rabbit tracks for much too long. They had to be reminded by its beginning to snow that it was time to go home. And the loggers' road back, all uphill and only broken by their own footsteps, took the longest of all. Jane thought some of the time that she would like to lie down and die comfortably in the warm snow. Edie and Widgy tried to until Ted kicked them quite hard. Before they were up the hill, Jane and Theodore had to take Edie by her hands and haul, because she did not seem to be able to raise her feet off the ground. And Widgy stopped quite a ways back and sat there goggle-eyed and panting. Hubert had to get him and give him a ride the rest of the way. They were so relieved to turn into the fir-lined road and see Mr. Carpenter's house at the end that for a few minutes it did not matter that there were still no tracks, no lights, and no glittering auto at its front door.

And there was no enormous crackling fire in the fire-place either, they found, as they pushed slowly into the darkened living room. The dry wood had burned quickly, and the cold and great open chimney letting the snow down had done the rest. They sat down in the half-dark because they had to, and they all looked desolately at the still blacker place where the fire had been.

"We'll start it again," said Theodore finally, getting up.

"What with?" said Jane.

There was only the enormous pile of big logs at one side of the fireplace. Mr. Wood had used up all the funny papers and also the kindling he had got out back.

"All right," said Theodore to Hubert. "You go look for it."

While he was gone, Jane rummaged in the box where the groceries were and found a big blue box of matches, and Theodore pushed the ashes apart, hoping to find a spark. They were still warm, but there was not a single glowing piece of anything. It was dead all right.

When Hubert came back, he said he had found an ice-house just beyond the kitchen door and that was all, so Ted went to look himself. But wherever Mr. Carpenter kept his kindling, it was not anywhere to be found in the midst of a snowstorm.

"Where's your knife?" Theodore said to Hubert when he came back. "I lost mine at school."

"That's just why I lent you mine," said Hubert. "Remember?"

Theodore put his hands in his pockets. The hole was still there in the right-hand one, but Hubert's knife was not. He hunched his shoulders and walked up and down. "This is serious," he said. "You can freeze in here. I advise you to help me get a fire started."

"Where *are* they?" said Jane furiously. "Why don't they *come?*"

"Confound you to everlasting," Theodore shouted. He had to howl at all these stupid kids. "Can't you think of something? Do you want to die?"

Edie began to whimper. "My feet are dead already nearly," she said.

"Go on and cry," said Theodore callously. "Yell! It'll keep you warm. Think!" he said to Jane and Hubert. "Think, you dumbheads!"

Hubert thought. "You could burn the house down maybe, but it might make Mr. Carpenter awfully mad."

Theodore snorted. "An ax," he said. "Gee, if we just had the smallest ax, we could cut some pieces off almost anywhere."

They wandered through the house forlornly by the light of bunches of matches looking for something they could break up and use, or something that had been left around, but Mr. Carpenter's house was absolutely tidy—no chips, no boards or old shingles were lying anywhere. The kitchen stove had a bucket of coal beside it, but they could not light that with a match. All the furniture seemed made of solid slabs.

"How about gnawing off a bit," said Hubert, setting his teeth in the back of a dining-room chair. He tried, but they slid off, and he only bit his tongue. They came back to the sitting room and started around it once more. Jane went over every piece with her eyes, carefully, as Theodore held up his little torch.

"Look!" she said.

She was pointing at a whole bookcase full of books.

"Quick," said Jane. "Make a pile of matches. We'll tear out pages and hand them to you. Hubert, maybe you *could* tear off some wood with your teeth. Those logs are different. Try it. Use your nails too."

They thought for a minute they were saved, although Theodore could not act as quickly as they wanted him to.

"Some books are valuable," he said, hooking one out.

"Not as valuable as lives," said Jane.

"All right," he said, shoving it at her. "Let's get started."

He made a small hollow in the warmest part of the

ashes and, taking a risk, put half his matches in it and
then on top several leaves from Mr. Carpenter's biggest
book. "Now!" he said, lighting the matches. They flared
up bravely, took hold of the paper, curled it up and turned
it black, and then died down and looked sick. "More!" he
said. "Hurry!" Jane handed him some more pages, and
Theodore fed them to the tiny dying flame, but it would
not have anything to do with them. He blew gently, and
the last of the matches curled up too and went out.

Hubert saw it with dismay. "Phew, what'll we do now?"
he said. "I never was so cold. The books must be about artic
voyages. Can't you find anything else, Jane?"

"We can't risk any more matches," said Theodore. "We'll
have to use paper alone. Here, give me lots of it. Edie, if
you don't stop that clatter with your teeth, I'll tie up your
jaw."

Jane gave him pages and pages, shiny and cold, that she
had fumbled for in the bookcase. They all wilted away
from Theodore's match without making a flame. She
scrambled over and got herself some matches to see what
she was doing.

"They *are* about artic voyages," she said, seeing a part of
a picture in the flare.

"And they're cold and damp naturally," said Hubert,
giving up trying to tear off bark for a minute and crawling
over to the bookcase. "Here, let me look." Jane's match
went out, and he had to wait till she lit another. "Hi, here's
French," he said like a cock crowing. "I bet that'll burn.
It's all about love." He pulled out some paper-backed books

and brought them on his hands and knees to the fireplace.

Theodore crumpled the French pages into a ball, put some of Hubert's gnawed chips on top, and tried again. This time the little delicate tongue of flame licked up healthily. Then it took hold of the bark and sizzled out.

"Do you have to drench those things with spit," Theodore said furiously.

"I don't know why," said Hubert, "but it just gets going if you gnaw. I wish I had one of those dentist things. Here, try these; they're drier."

Theodore waited this time until he had balls and balls of French paper ready. Then they all went at a log except Edie, who was holding her chin with her hand, and presently in the pitch dark each had a few scraps of bark in each hand. Theodore collected them by feeling and placed them, also by feeling, carefully spaced on the paper. Then he lit the pile.

"You'd better pray," he said. "There's only three matches left."

The flame ran along the edges of the paper and didn't do anything. Weakly and feebly it ran inside a ball and disappeared. As it went Jane, who had forgotten the cold, began to feel it like knives on her skin, as if it had cut through her clothes. Theodore leaned over to see what had happened, and just then the fire gave a little pouf and the whole pile of paper sprang alight at once.

"Boy!" said Theodore. Then he pounded on the hearthstone. "Give me some more, quick, more. Tear it small.

GIVE ME MORE," he roared. He fed and fed the fire until the chips gave a slight crackle and the flame, although it did not look very healthy, was quite tall and reaching for something more to eat.

"Give it a whole French book," said Hubert.

"NO," said Theodore. He jumped to his feet. "Holy mackerel," he said. "We've got to have something GOOD." He looked wildly round the room. He looked at Widgy, who was half under a table, as if he might use him. Jane looked too and saw what Widgy was doing.

"That's it," she shrieked. "It's got a straw top, hurry."

Theodore picked up the little footstool that Widgy had tugged forward and placed it neatly over the lessening flame. The tip was just tall enough to reach the straw, and it caught. He crammed more paper under it and it caught, and he gave it more and more until the whole footstool was blazing. When it was going hard, and at just the right moment, he and Hubert picked up a large log and carefully and reverently laid it across the top. Then they all kneeled on the hearthstone and waited to see if the fire would take hold.

"That was a close thing," said Theodore, as the flames closed round the log. "A very close thing. Now," he said, "close all the doors, and we'll get up a good heat in here."

There was plenty of big wood, and the boys kept piling it on until the whole giant fireplace was flaming. They sat in front of it and baked and, when their clothes began to steam, took them off and hung them on the fender. They lugged their suitcases out of the cold in the hall and warmed them up and then changed their socks and baked some more, seeing how near they could come to broiling the soles of their feet. Widgy crawled out of Edie's arms and lay on the hearth and panted. He looked so happy that Jane and Hubert and Edie stretched out too and tried panting a little with him. Theodore lay on his back and stared at the ceiling, remembering the cold. Presently he said: "Where are those groceries? I'm hungry."

The grocery box had been left in the entry and was very cold indeed, but for some reason they would never know, nothing was frozen, and unloading it was a great deal better than Christmas. First there was bread, then butter, then jam. There were also flour and sugar and salt and pepper. These they put on the table to have them out of the way. Then there was a chocolate cake, and Theodore found some sausages.

"There must," he said almost solemnly as he jounced them in his hand, "be some way to cook these things or they wouldn't have sent them. Suppose we have a look."

When he came back from the next room, where he felt about in the dark with his hands, he had a frying pan.

"We can use the poker to stir 'em up," he said.

What they then ate was a feast. Hubert began with fig newtons and chocolate cake because he had always wanted to eat a meal backwards. He finished with sausages and jam. Jane toasted her bread, slathered it with butter by means of the poker, and took alternate bites with her sausage. Theodore seemed to eat everything at once, and Edie collected a supply for herself and Widgy and then fell over asleep. Widgy finished it all off.

"And now," said Theodore with an enormous swallow over the last bite, "for a bottle of beer."

"Just what I was thinking," said Hubert.

"Don't do it," said Jane.

She did not know exactly what she expected to happen if the boys drank beer. But she thought they might begin to dance and sing or something frightful.

"And why not, old Mrs. Widow O'Warty?" said Hubert freshly, just as if he had gotten drunk at the mere thought of it.

They had a hard time getting the tops off the bottles, and that was a good thing for half the beer spilled out. Widgy licked it up immediately and instead of dancing and singing lay down and went sound asleep. And this, it turned out, was exactly what happened to Hubert and Theodore. They got a little red and tried a little teasing, but all of a sudden their eyelids began to close.

"It's been a hard day, old man," said Theodore and stretched himself out.

"It's been a hard day, old man yourself," said Hubert and lay back.

Jane leaned back on her hands and looked around. The room was a mess of clothes, paper, scraps, food, especially chocolate cake, packages, and right by the boys' noses, empty bottles of beer. As she was looking at it, the door latch rattled, so that she turned round with a jump to look. There, standing in the door, was Mr. Carpenter. She looked at him and Mr. Carpenter looked at the mess. They had certainly broken training. *What* was he going to say?

Mr. Carpenter pursed up his lips and stuck them forward. "Alive, I see. Stout lads."

Jane thought these words were delightful. She stepped over Edie's curled-up body when Mr. Carpenter beckoned her and followed him out to the porch. It was still snowing, and there was no auto by the steps.

"Where's Father?" Jane asked.

Mr. Carpenter rose up and down on his toes.

"Your respected male parent," he said, "has developed a most horrendous cold and has gone to bed at the inn in the village."

Jane found it impossible to say anything. She had thought they were halfway to the frozen North.

"Where's the auto?" she asked rather feebly.

"Ah," said Mr. Carpenter, "you pluck at my heart-strings."

Although they stayed at the house for five whole days and found out that Mr. Carpenter had beds, blankets, more gigantic fireplaces, more wood, lots of kindling, lamps galore if you knew where to look for them, they never found out very much about what had happened to him and Father and the auto. They did not see the auto, and they did not see Father until they gathered him up with Mr. Wood's milk sleigh on the way to the train back to Summerton.

They did not think about him either if they could help it.
To have to see him between the wan white sheets of a bed,
sneezing his head off, made him into a regular baby. Instead they did all the things they had been told they had
to do in the Far North and some more besides. Hubert
learned to make flapjacks, Theodore went trapping on the
river, Edie and Widgy almost caught a rabbit, and all of
them chopped in the woods with real axes or hatchets and
built gigantic bonfires. They only washed once a day, and
they slept in most of their clothes. They agreed that they
could not possibly see how anyone could be afraid of the
frozen North. Not if there was fire.

But picking up Father was another thing. It was embarrassing. He was done up right to his ears in coats and scarfs,
and his cap was pulled down as far as it would go. And it
was really quite a warm day. The Cares were all boiling.
They did not really see him until they were on the train,
but they listened with great respect to his cough, and when
they were comfortably settled and he was unwrapped, they
had to think respectfully of how sick he had been.

This time there would not have been any funny papers
if it had not been for Mr. Carpenter. Father did not buy
anything but a paper for himself. But Mr. Carpenter, just
as the train was leaving, put a funny paper in each child's
lap and sat back chewing and smiling as if he were pleased.

"Harry," said Father, "you're an old humbug."

"Oh, no," said Jane violently, before she could stop herself. "Not *him*."

Everyone was dreadfully silent.

"Every time you open your mouth, you put your foot in it," said Theodore graciously from across the aisle.

"Well, so am I!" said Father after a minute, with a gesture of his hands as if he gave up.

Nobody looked up, but each Cares smiled a little at the others from under their eyebrows while Father took up his paper and began to read.

CHAPTER FIVE

The Horticultural Ball

The end of the Christmas vacation was also the end of the school that had pleased Hubert in Canboro—at least for him. Out of the blue, Father sent for him to come to the study and told him the news. Nobody could think of a reason for the change, and nobody could think of anything bad that Hubert had done. He had annoyed Father a few times, that was all, by building a nest in the downstairs closet where the light was good and reading the funny papers there with a bottle of root beer on his stomach. He had thought innocently that he would be out of everyone's way. But Father had stumbled over him when he put his coat away. So now it was decided that the thing to do with him so that he would not continue to be corrupted by root beer and luxury was to send him to a school in Charlottesville— a real school where there were boys who spent their spare time not in coat closets, but "in the discipline of the fray," Father had explained.

"But I have a good school," said Hubert crossly to Theodore and Jane when he came out of the study. Theodore had been practicing golf on the red carpet of the front hall with a mashie, and Hubert got down on his hands and knees to put back the pile divots for him.

"He means football and that sort of thing," said Jane, slapping her scrapbook shut and sitting on it so that the pictures she had been pasting would stay down. "You shouldn't have told him they let you get out of it at Canboro."

Hubert didn't mind football, he said; what he minded was having his face stepped on.

"Are you going to live at this school?" asked Jane.

"I'm living with my sister at my grandfather's," said Hubert. "How do you like that?" Jane liked it very well, but she could not help feeling for Hubert for having to do it.

Theodore considered a loose piece of red fluff. "You sit too much on that fat tail of yours," he said, taking a tremendous swing.

"And you don't sit enough on that fat head of *yours,*" said Hubert quickly. He moved away as fast as he could, but he was not quite fast enough, and he was in a very convenient position. When he was getting ready for bed, Jane had to admire his black-and-blue spot.

"It was worth it, though," he said, jerking his pajama cord tight. "He tripped over the mashie and broke it, and I called him a fathead to the very end."

His satisfaction did not last through till the morning, however. By that time an unusual quiet had descended on Hubert. Jane could not understand it. It had snowed again, but he would not go punging or fix the fort or roll snowballs or find drifts to jump in or even try sliding down the

slippery barn roof. Life, he argued, was full of danger
enough as it was. You couldn't even live in your own house
these days without running into it. While he was standing
irresolutely under the porte-cochère, Jane offered to clean
up Gwendolyn with him. But Hubert was not going to
spend his last few precious days on a silly pigeon. He
scrunched himself together at the very idea of the cold hay-
loft and pigeon cote.

"Maybe she's laid an egg," said Jane encouragingly,
standing beside him. "And we could keep her from eating
it." Almost any time you could get Hubert excited by this
idea, but not today.

"She's too old," he said. "Anyway, I'm not interested in
cannibals. I feel like a cannibal myself."

"I suppose you'd like to eat Father," said Jane understandingly. Hubert thought maybe he would. "But not his
mustache," he said after thinking it over. In the end he
wandered off to the Reservoir by himself. He thought the
sight of a wild animal would be the only thing that would
do him any good.

Hubert's silence lasted a long time and was very inconvenient. He still had it on the way into town on the Sunday afternoon train, which they were allowed to take alone
if they promised to go to Grandfather's in one of Bishop's
cabs. He went, silently, with Jane to shake hands with
Grandfather, he climbed the stairs to the third floor where
his room was next to Jane's, kicking every tread, and he
put back his head and looked at the gas lighting contemp-

tuously. Jane showed him the window that looked out at
the backyard.

"There are a lot of cat fights out there," she said.

Hubert looked at the darkness without answering.

Jane led him back to the living room where Grandfather
was and pushed him into a chair. There was one thing
about Grandfather, he always treated them as if he did not
know they were there. They could see that he was alive
himself by the smoke that kept coming up from behind his
newspaper and by the occasional movement of one of his
smooth leather boots, but he only appeared in real life at
mealtimes or just before they went to bed. It was all he
could stand, they supposed, but it was nice for them too.
Jane was able to look at Hubert and let her own disgust
begin to boil up. "All right," she said, "have a grouch if
you want, but I think you're a pill."

Hubert looked at his boots sadly. He was not having a
grouch or trying to be a pill in the least. He was like the
Spartan boy, and had a fox eating his insides. He had not
told her everything that Father had said in the study; the
worst was yet to come.

"What?" asked Jane.

"Did you realize," said Hubert, sitting up, "that we not
only have to go to school in this place, but that we are
going to be made into ladies and gentlemen?"

"Ha, ha," said Jane suddenly. "I don't see how they're
going to do that."

"Don't you?" said Hubert. "How about a thing like
dancing school?"

Jane flung herself back in her chair. He was making it up, of course, because he was in a mean mood. Hubert did not deign to answer.

"How do you *know?*" she said, feeling weaker.

"Aunt Charlotte fixed it with Father," said Hubert plain and simply.

Jane had to become silent herself and look at her own boots sadly.

This was because she knew, and all of them knew, that Aunt Charlotte was just like Fate. You might be able to avoid her for a certain length of time, but in the end she talked to Father and Father listened. How he could, his children could never see. She was his sister, that was true, but to the boys that made it more astounding still, and Jane had her own thoughts. If she were Father, she could not imagine being able to stand what Aunt Charlotte said about her children. But he had his own reasons. At least he said so often.

"Your Aunt Charlotte does so much for you children." That was one of them.

Last summer when Theodore, purely accidentally, put his foot in one of her flower beds getting a baseball, they had all, while they had helped him work out his sentence of raking the lawn, tried honestly and carefully to count up their blessings from Aunt Charlotte.

"Edie's costume from Paris for one," said Hubert.

But this had not been much use to Edie. It had had a hat like a bowl made of lace, and a coat of cherry-colored silk. She had fallen down in a mud puddle with it just after it had been put on, and it was never seen again.

"Why should a life so brief," Theodore had wondered, throwing out his rake like a net on the lawn sea, "require so much gratitude?"

"And don't forget the hat she brought you, Jane," Edie had said.

Oh, yes, that was another thing. Jane's hat had come from Paris too and been enormous. It was the biggest hat anyone in the Cares family had ever seen, or, Hubert said, would ever want to see. It had been made of bright red straw, and it had a yellow bow blazing out in front. Jane, who never wore a hat, except her sailor to go to church with Grandfather, had had to put this on instead. Miraculously it had also disappeared, but not in a mud puddle. Jane sometimes thought it might have been Grandfather. He had looked at her as she got into the beech wagon and remarked, "What's that you've got on your head?"

"She told me to keep my mouth shut when I chewed," said Theodore, doing his best to rake up Edie.

"That's a blessing all right," said Hubert, moving back. "But I made a good joke once, and she said I was showing off."

"I picked the smallest bunch of lilies of the valley on earth," said Jane, "and she sent me to Father for stealing."

So it was clear in Grandfather's living room that Hubert had a right to have a grouch. Jane wanted to do something. Not plead with Father, of course, that would be useless, but ask Madam, write Theodore, get Grandfather on their side, rouse the populace like in the French Revolution.

"Go ahead," said Hubert. "You'll just bump your nose on a lot of stony elbows. There's no use fighting Fate. I'm going to forget the whole thing." He would not answer any further questions about when Fate would be overtaking them or what they would have to do, or how many times, or where. Now that the horrible news was off his mind, he meant to begin forgetting right away.

He did not have any trouble doing it. After dinner, meandering through the second floor, he discovered Grandfather's letter-weigher and fell in love with it. Jane knew it well. It had two little gold platforms, and the weights were little gold lumps that looked like cakes. She had been in love with it herself before Christmas. For nights and nights Hubert weighed whatever he could find that was small enough, and as only the dollhouse had a lot of these, he fell in love with that too. Jane sat cross-legged in front of him making things out of paper. It was the one good thing inherited from Mademoiselle. Mademoiselle had known how to make almost anything out of colored paper by cutting and folding the right way, and Jane could remember most of them. Neither of them did any homework. "We slog for them for six hours," said Hubert. "That's enough." Jane agreed. She did not know where there would have been time for it anyway. As Hubert's hostess she was very busy. She had to show him how to fire oranges out the dining-room window when Grandfather had been disturbed by cats; she had to pull him up and down in the dumb-waiter; and as soon as he was a little less in love with his gold cakes, she taught him how ·to bounce marbles from the window onto the sidewalk. If it was done right, they sprang into the air and landed sometimes on the top of a cab and from there sometimes on a horse.

"Gee, Jane," said Hubert, ducking behind the casement after a particularly good shot that had made people stop and stare, "this is so decent a boy might have thought of it."

Jane nodded. She herself thought she was doing pretty well.

With all these things to fill the time, it was easy to forget Fate for a few days. But It did not forget you, not if It was Aunt Charlotte. As the plan for dancing school developed, it was worse than they had dreamed. At three o'clock on Thursdays they had to take baths in the middle of the day, dress in stiff clothes, and be driven by one of Bishop's cabs to their doom, which was a brightly lighted room with gilded chairs in Charlottesville's best hotel. Hubert had to wear a stiff collar besides his stiff clothes. Jane moaned in sympathy before she knew what Aunt Charlotte had advised about herself.

"The child's hair will have to be properly done," she said to Father. "She can't go looking like an Indian."

On Wednesday nights Nellie Flaherty began winding up Jane's hair in damp strips of cotton so that the next day she would have a mop of corkscrew curls. Hubert did not moan. He kept coming to the door and going away with his hand over his mouth. Jane hated him almost as much as Aunt Charlotte for a while and prayed for God to let

her be a poisonous snake and give both of them—One
Good Bite.

He did not do this for her, and He did not stop time and
the world so that Thursday would never come, as she also
asked Him to be good enough to do. On the contrary, He
arranged to have Aunt Charlotte herself come to see if they
were properly dressed.

She stood them up in the hall and made them put out
their hands. Hubert was sent upstairs to clean his nails,
and Jane had to have her hair ribbon twitched and opened
out.

"It looks like a boat's main sheet all right," said Hubert
on the way to the hall.

From the moment they got there, they hardly knew how
to behave. The hall was full of boys and girls they had
never seen before, dressed like themselves in uncomfortable
clothes, and in the middle of them was Miss Pepper. Miss
Pepper was an old lady—she had gray hair!—but she acted
so young and foolish it was a shame to look at her. She
skipped, she ran with little steps and slides, she clapped her
hands, and she called out in a voice that sounded just like
Edie's. Hubert, although he resisted with dumb paralysis,
was suddenly picked up and whirled away by her while
she hummed in his ear. Jane, in the Grand March, found
herself all alone at the end of the line. Her partner had es-
caped when no one was looking and had joined someone
up forward he liked better.

The moment they got back to Grandfather's they did
their best. Hubert left his blue suit in a heap in the middle

of his room and rolled on the floor. He said he was taking a dust bath. If that was good for a hen's itch, it might be good for his. Jane dipped her curled head deep in the bathroom basin. Still, what was the good? Thursday came round every week almost as if it were the only day there was. The only scrap of hope anywhere was the Easter vacation, and that was a million years away. Further than that even. They did not know it yet, but vacation was on the other side of the Horticultural Ball.

The Horticultural Ball was what Aunt Charlotte had decided was to be at the end of dancing school. As Theodore said, the torture chamber. Because Ted, as well as Jane and Hubert, on the Friday night before they went home, was to stop off in the city to escort Aunt Charlotte to this festivity. Word was brought to Jane and Hubert by Grandfather. He put down his paper one evening at the end of March and said: "I hear you are attending a rout."

"We are?" they asked.

"Your aunt," said Grandfather, "has asked me to extend you this invitation." He took a large square card off his side table and handed it to them.

"It doesn't say anything about a riot here," said Hubert. "It just says dancing. Do we have to go?"

"I believe your aunt is counting on it," said Grandfather. He looked at them over the lowered part of his paper. "What, if I may be permitted to inquire, are you planning to wear?"

Jane looked at him doubtfully. "Clothes, I suppose," she said.

Hubert handed him back the card politely by its very edge. "That's what I planned too," he said.

Grandfather shook his paper out straight before he began reading again. "It's my impression," he said, "that you will be expected to appear in disguise." He covered himself up again. "Your aunt," he said reading from the very top of his paper, "may not be wholly unwise."

That's all they got out of Grandfather. It took Nellie Flaherty a long time to convince them that their aunt had arranged a lovely treat for them and their big brother and that they were to be at her city house at seven-thirty on the twenty-fifth of March so that they could dress up and enjoy it. It was not until they went home for the week end that they could believe their ears. Hubert explained frankly that he thought he was far too young for so much responsibility, and Jane, though she did not dare to say anything, looked what she was thinking—that girls were no good at balls anyhow. They might as well have tried to stop a railroad train or change the moon. Father, when he saw that Madam did not like the looks on their faces, told them to take them away where they could not be seen. Nobody thought of removing the Horticultural Ball instead.

During the next week, when a big sheet of paper in a still bigger envelope arrived in Grandfather's mail for them, they knew Theodore had been told. The paper had one word on it. It said: "Idiots."

"He thinks we got him into it," said Jane.

Theodore did think this, and the way he bounced his bag down in the hall as soon as he got to Grandfather's

on the afternoon of the ball made them sure of it. They
were being as quiet as mice in the dollhouse room. Silence,
they hoped, might possibly have some effect on the raging
of a lion. But Theodore crashed himself and his bag upstairs and roared it away.

"Will you please explain how you managed to get us
into such a confounded, unmitigated, unholy, everlasting
mess?" he said.

Jane and Hubert concentratedly weighed the dollhouse
tables and chairs as if they had not heard, and strangely
enough Ted seemed to exhaust himself with one roar. He
sat down hard on the sofa and hung his whole body down
between his knees.

"What do we have to do?"

Hadn't he been told? Jane and Hubert swung round
brightly. They had to wear costumes and go to the Horticultural Ball with Aunt Charlotte.

"What as?"

They didn't know any more than he did. There were to
be things at her house for them to put on.

"What's *she* going as?"

They didn't know that either. "God, no doubt," said
Hubert.

He may have thought of this because Aunt Charlotte's
house was something like heaven—grand, good-smelling,
and silent as the grave, like it said in hymns at church.
It made them feel as if *they* must be good, not just their
own kind of goodness, but Aunt Charlotte's. It made them
almost *want* to be, especially the hall, where the great wide

easy staircase went sweeping up and swung round to the second floor as if it owned everything and yet left plenty of room. There was a great dark wood table at one side and on the other a whole garden of trees and flowers. Carefully and dignifiedly, they took off their coats and handed them to the man who had let them in. His name was Eliot, and they knew he was Aunt Charlotte's butler, but they would not have thought of being familiar enough to speak to the man who was in charge of heaven. On tiptoe they walked into the enormous shadowed room beyond the hall. There was not much of it to be seen—only two black velvet sofas and two round scarlet cushions and a blue hippopotamus on a table, but lighted by two lamps and a blazing fire the space made a little room of its own. Upstairs, they knew, among her satins and window boxes Aunt Charlotte's house always smelled of spring, but here perhaps it was like wood and roses. It had the same effect on them all. It made them sit on the edge of the black velvet sofas wondering how they could be as wonderful as what was around them. It had another effect, too. They had to hope they would not grow any bigger while they were there. Even though Aunt Charlotte's house was so quietly lit, everything about them seemed to show more in it, everything about them got bigger, except their brains. They could feel *them* shrinking.

One of the reasons for this was that they knew they would presently have to say something. Instead of liking peace and quiet at meals like Father, Aunt Charlotte liked conversation.

"I'm stumped if I know what to say to her," said Theodore getting up and trying hard to breathe through his nose. "Does anybody remember what she knows anything about?"

"Shhhhhhh," said Jane.

"She knows about art, books, flowers, and how to behave in the house," said Hubert in a voice you could hardly hear. "That's more than we know." He moved a little nearer the edge of the sofa.

"Try her on fire engines, thoroughbred horses, and the Repertory Theater and see how you come out," said Theodore.

"Shhhhhh," said Jane. "She's coming."

They got themselves together in order to have their muscles ready for politeness while eating dinner with Aunt Charlotte. They did not need them for the food. There was nothing the matter with that! Or the dining room either, with its great silver candlesticks and the paintings on its walls. No one but Aunt Charlotte ever had such paintings that they knew of. They blazed out from the darkness. Houses were orange, trees were apple green, grass was yellow, streets were rose and bright brown. But the food and the paintings did for Jane and Hubert. They found their brains had disappeared altogether. And Theodore, when he tried some little thing about the weather, knocked a serving spoon with potato onto the table so that it rang like a bell. He would gladly have wiped it up himself with a clean handkerchief, but when he tried, he bumped his

head on Eliot who had got there before him, and he had
to watch him scraping away with a knife and small plate.
Their muscles for conversation refused to move after that.
And Aunt Charlotte's conversation, as far as they could see,
did not come up to scratch either. It was mostly about the
manners of the modern day.

"We don't seem to know much about them," said Jane
meekly, so as to calm her down.

Aunt Charlotte asked Hubert what he knew about music. Luckily he had his mouth full, and while she was waiting, she let her eyes rest on Ted.

"Not much and that's a fact," he said boldly.

"I was just trying to liven things up a bit," he explained
afterwards.

"Well, you didn't," said Hubert. "She looked as if she
was quietly and calmly having a fit."

After dinner they were given a little while in the library
to converse about their schools. They tried with all their
might. Jane said she had a desk mate who did not like her,
Hubert admitted that he was not good at football, and Theodore told her that one of the masters at his school had a
"down" on him.

"We don't seem too popular, I admit," he added apologetically.

Aunt Charlotte looked at them each in turn. "You
should make yourselves so useful and attractive you would
be," she said, stirring her coffee hard.

In spite of what was in front of them, it was a relief to

be told to go up to the third floor and put on their costumes. The maid would be there, Aunt Charlotte said, and she herself would come and get them later.

"What are we?" Theodore managed to ask through the bars of the golden elevator cage in the back hall as it started to go up.

"You're laid out on the bed," said Aunt Charlotte, her voice and head going up with the elevator. "You will see for yourselves."

They did see, but not for themselves. Aunt Charlotte's maid had to explain. What was there for Theodore and Jane seemed to be a pair of nightgowns.

"Cleopâtre pour Mademoiselle," said Amlie. *"Et voici votre belle bandeau avec des cheveux noirs."* She held up a golden band with tight black curls hanging from it. Jane stared.

"Et pour Monsieur Téodor, César," said Amlie triumphantly. *"Il a aussi une jolie chose pour la tête."* And there was Caesar's toga and a crown of laurel leaves for Ted. He stared too.

Hubert did not have to be told. He took one look and knew. So did Theodore, and the influence of Aunt Charlotte's house went up in smoke. "Little Boy Blue come blow your horn," said Ted. "Or I'm a melon."

"Say that again," said Hubert instantly, "and I'll knock your block off."

"Take a try," said Theodore, facing round and getting his fists ready, "go on, take a small poke."

Jane had to put her hands over her middle. They had been commanded to come here by Father. Madam had no sympathy with them. Their conversation downstairs had not made a very good impression, and now the boys were going to fight all over Aunt Charlotte's best guest room. She was scared. She saw Amlie scuttle out the door and heard her say: *"Mon Dieu!"* She did not see Aunt Charlotte come in until Hubert got a tap on the head with a slim black cane.

"Hey," said Hubert sharply. He turned and rocked on his heels with his arm pulled back, and for a second it looked as if he was going to take a swipe at Aunt Charlotte. But Jane guessed no one could take a look at her and go on fighting. She had only got as far in her dressing as a gold crown. The rest of her was in a wrapper. (And it made you think of what Hubert had said!) It stopped the fight, it even, when she had gone back to her room, made them turn silently to their costumes and ask Amlie sulkily how you got the darn things on.

In spite of her enthusiastic help, getting dressed was a great deal of trouble. Theodore would not take off his pants no matter what room he was given to do it in, and he was going to wear his own boots. He was cold, he said. Rome had had a warmer climate. Hubert had been made so reckless by rage that he was willing to take off everything right there. He had to be shoved into a closet. Jane, with the thought that somebody better do something, if only to get away alive, tried to cram Cleopatra's wig over her thick light braids. It was no use. It made her look like a pumpkin, as the boys soon told her. She had to stick her hair down her neck and let it itch there.

When they were ready, Aunt Charlotte, in a red velvet robe and purple gown, came and gazed at them. She found something missing. It could not have been Theodore's boots because they were easy enough to see under his toga, and it could not have been any part of Hubert because every bit of him showed. Whatever part of Jane might not be there was covered with yards of white drapery. Aunt Charlotte, it seemed, meant their faces. They were to hold up their heads and look proud, and she walked back and forth to show them what she meant. At the door she stopped and told the boys they might pick up her train and they would all proceed. The moment had come. Julius Caesar, Boy Blue, and Cleopatra Cares were now going out to be seen in public. In the carriage they kept their coats hugged round them. It was snowing gently, but hard, on the way to the Horticultural Ball. Aunt Charlotte's prancing horses might easily have fallen down on the slippery pavement, but probably horses do not understand mental telepathy, because they high-stepped down the Concourse without a fault.

In the dark safety of Aunt Charlotte's box—her private recessed seats—before the future was revealed to him, Hubert had the thought that if he could have been a fly he might have been glad to come to a Horticultural Ball. In that case he could have watched everything with dozens of eyes. This was the way, if he ever got the chance, he would build a giant's palace—all those lights and glittering golden decorations, all those mirrors flashing out flowers, and all those people covered with colors. He would remember right here and now as much as he could. It was too bad that at the same time he remembered himself and his bright blue satin. But he could fix that. Cautiously, with his toes, he moved his chair back a little. Theodore and Jane glanced in his direction instantly. They moved their chairs back a little too. There was a steady slow retreat of golden chairs in Aunt Charlotte's box under cover of the crashing orchestra. But before they could all get into the really deep shadow beyond the corner of Aunt Charlotte's eye, the door at the back of the box opened and a devil came in.

There was no one of the Cares children who especially disapproved of devils, but who should this one turn out to be? That skunk of a Willy McHenry! Living across the road from him in Summerton all their lives, they knew exactly what he was like. Besides, Boney, his younger sister, had always been glad to give them extra information. Theodore and Hubert were about the most obnoxious little kids he knew, and Jane was "damn plain." Edie—well, Edie— Willy sometimes wondered if the kid was all there. And here he was showing off in a dandy devil's costume at the Horticultural Ball. The Cares looked simultaneously and raptly down at their own knees, and they all became as still as statues. Perhaps he would go away. But no such luck. After speaking to Aunt Charlotte as if he knew everything in the world about politeness, he made a bow in front of

Jane. The cheek! At the same time Aunt Charlotte turned halfway round in her chair. Hubert gave Jane a poke because she didn't move.

"Go on," he said from the side of his mouth, "you have to do something."

At least he and Theodore were saved.

"Here," said Aunt Charlotte suddenly, "take these two boys with you. I want them to dance."

When they reached the crowded floor of the ballroom, there was just one hope left. Willy might not be able to find them someone to dance with. But the hope was forlorn. Willy was an usher and knew where the girls were kept. There was a regular pool of them down at one end of the room. The boys saw them at the same time.

"I guess I'll dance with Jane," said Hubert like lightning, dodging in front of her.

"No, I will," said Theodore, dodging in front of *him* and making the bow Hubert had forgotten. "Hurry," he said to Jane between his teeth.

But Jane was not going to have anything to do with *them,* the traitors. She would not raise her arms.

"Not a chance," said Willy cheerfully and turned them forcefully by pinching their shoulders. Theodore he presented with a kind of Alice-in-Wonderland, who was sitting with her mother under a palm tree, and for Hubert he got some sort of small animal that looked like a mouse. She wasn't bad as far as her face was concerned, but her fur pricked when he tried to take hold of her.

"Are you a mole, by any chance?" asked Hubert, as he

tried to get going. It was something he thought that might interest him.

"Yes," said the animal.

"Well, you shouldn't have eyes," said Hubert. "Moles are blind."

The mole did not answer. And no wonder; she did not know how to dance at all. At least not in any way that Miss Pepper had ever heard of. Miss Pepper wanted steps taken with care and grace. The mole hopped. She did not know or seem to care what happened to Hubert. Wherever he put down his feet, hers were there first. He really did not think that this could be dancing, so he tried something else. He hopped too. And it seemed to him as if he had never undertaken anything so hard, so hot, and so shameful. This mole was a baby. He didn't believe she had ever been out on a dance floor before. Working like anything, he tried to see Theodore and Jane. He caught a glimpse of them briefly. Willy was using Jane as a battering-ram while he galloped up and down, and Ted was hardly moving, just turning Alice round and round. Hubert envied him deeply. As usual Ted was managing to have his own way. But the next time he saw him he realized there might be a reason for it. Theodore's toga had slipped. Every time he took a step it was getting under his boots. Whenever he was bumped by somebody, he staggered. The next time Hubert saw him he stopped hopping and let go of the mole. Someone had given Ted an extra hard push, and he was taking a long step to get back his balance. He should not have done it. The next minute he was walking up his toga

toward his neck while Alice-in-Wonderland skipped neatly
out of the way. In another second he was going to fall flat.
Hubert bent backwards and Ted had some luck. His toga
gave a loud rip and slipped to his feet. Thank the Lord, if
you could say such a thing, Hubert thought, because there
was Julius Caesar at the Horticultural Ball in a singlet and
knickerbockers. Very few people could see him on account of the crowd, but the ones that could began to
laugh. Willy McHenry bellowed, and Hubert's mole gave a
titter. He turned and fixed *her*. He put a satin knee in the
middle of her fur stomach and sat her down hard. Then
he got ready to charge. If he knew Ted, he would have to
fight the whole ballroom, and this time Hubert meant to
die at his side.

This did not happen, though. Theodore stood still a minute, held up his laurel-leaf crowned head, gave the toga a
kick, glared at everybody, and then began to stalk across
the room. The dancers made way for him and for Hubert
and for Jane, who picked up the toga as she went by. Theodore made for the first door in sight. It was a long way
from Aunt Charlotte's box, but they walked round the circular outside corridor as if no one was there. Hubert, after
a skip or two, matched his stride to Ted's. Jane came behind with Cleopatra's skirts in her hand. At the door of
the box Hubert had a kind of convulsion, and after it was
over, he threw his blue satin tunic back to Jane. Then
they opened the door and went in. Softly and silently they
took their golden chairs and sat down. They saw that Aunt

Charlotte suspected nothing at all. She had not even been able to see what had happened. She began to speak graciously to her unexpected guest.

"There's been some kind of unpleasant rumpus," she said, pointing her fan to the far end of the room. "Can you tell me what it is? Has someone intoxicated had to be removed?"

No one answered.

Aunt Charlotte raised her voice slightly. "There has been a disturbance of some disgraceful kind—" She turned to her visitor. But she reared back as she saw that there were two of them and that they were both in their underclothes.

It got them away from the Horticultural Ball. And from Aunt Charlotte. The carriage was sent for, and they were led to it and put in by Willy McHenry, who came round, naturally, to enjoy everything. He made them a low bow with his hand on his heart as he closed the door and Fabian started the horses. They regretted forever that he could not see what they made to him with their hands on their stomachs inside the cab.

Once back in Aunt Charlotte's guest rooms Julius Caesar, Cleopatra, and Boy Blue flew in every direction. While the satin tunic was on the way down from the ceiling, Hubert caught it on his toe and sent it up to the mantelpiece. The blue hat with the feather he sailed into the bathtub right through the door like a bird on the wing. Jane and Theodore were more subdued. They wanted to go to bed; Ted was shivering and colder than ever.

"You shouldn't expose yourself so in public," said Hubert with grandeur as he went to get the feathered hat to see if he could do it again.

As they sat on the floor eating the crackers and milk that Amlie had left for them, he really became quite a nuisance. He wanted, he said, pounding his fist on the floor, to take revenge.

"Just how," asked Theodore, coughing, "are you going to do that?"

Hubert didn't know. He had to think. But no matter what happened to them afterwards he was sure that tonight they should have some sort of revenge.

"What's happened to *you* all of a sudden," asked Jane. She had never seen Hubert so brightly fierce.

Hubert could not have told. He had only felt this way once before in his life. That was when Boney McHenry had got him down, sat on the middle of his back, and made him eat dirt, because she had not been strong enough to do it to Theodore. Then he had been helpless, but now—For no reason that he knew of, he remembered the tailor in the *Blue Fairy Book* who had swatted seven flies at a blow. Hubert found it hard to have reasons. He usually left that to Jane. But he knew his wants very well. Right now he wanted to be like the tailor and get seven at one good blow. Possibly Aunt Charlotte and Boney might be among them.

"Let's cut all the heads off her flowers," he suggested. It would be delightful slashing away.

"No!" said Jane.

She and Ted began to yawn. They wouldn't agree to doing anything no matter how good an idea it was. There was nothing they could do, they said, without being found out, and they were in enough trouble already. They would just have to listen to Father until he got tired, apologize to Aunt Charlotte, and then probably go to reform school.

"I won't go without revenge," said Hubert.

He might be able to stand things for himself, but not for Ted, and not for all men and boys world without end. It made him feel as if he had swallowed a lot of stones.

As soon as Theodore crawled into bed still shivering—although Jane and Hubert told him he was as red as a lobster and couldn't be cold—Hubert crawled into his own. He listened to Ted snorting and chattering until this stopped and then got up and crept on his hands and knees to the door. "Seven at a blow," he said to himself as he let himself out.

The house was a flood of silence and darkness. He did not mind that. And he soon found it was not quite totally dark after all. The great windows were white from the street lights that seemed to make the rooms milk-white like the moon. What he did mind were the creaks from the stairs. They went off like pistol shots. He could hardly keep to his errand. But he was steadied by having thought, while Ted was composing himself for slumber, what he was going to do. His mind had gone all over the house searching for something with seven, and after a while he had found it.

Hubert kept on through the hall, through the dining

room, where he had to grope a bit, to the pantry door, which he pushed with one hand outstretched to get a look at it before he went in. It was completely black inside. He would have to have a light. It was too bad, he *loved* the blackness, but he must see to work. He turned the knob that made Aunt Charlotte's new 'lectricity come on and began to move a little faster than usual. Opening one of the glass cabinets where the dishes were kept, he gave himself just a hurried moment to study them. He decided on a pile of small plates on the lowest shelf and slipped them off. When he had counted out seven, he put the rest back, closed the cabinet without a sound, turned the wonderful 'lectricity off, and tiptoed out to the hall. Now was the hard part, but thinking of the tailor, he hoped to be able to do it. Setting the plates noiselessly on the hall table, he scrabbled in the closet under the stairs for his outdoor things. He was not sure he got his own, but he got somebody's, and they were good enough.

Hubert did not forget anything. He snapped the lock on Aunt Charlotte's front door so it would open for him on the way back, and as soon as he was outside he studied his direction. It was still snowing—no, it was snowing more and more, and it had been ever since they started for the Horticultural Ball; not in a wild blowing winter blizzard, but quiet, thick snow. That's what had made the rooms so full of white light! It made Charlottesville the most beautiful sight he had ever seen. But he could not stop for that now. No one was in sight, no one anyway that he could see through the snow. Or that could see him! In spite of having to be rather sedate on account of two hands full of

plates, it did not take him long to get to the park and to
the bridge over its pond. There he put the plates on the
parapet, where they sank into the snow, and looked to
either side. Still nobody. Hallelujah, every person in the
city and all the policemen had gone to bed. The snow came
down around him as if it would put him to bed too, but not
before he had finished his errand! Get ready, set, go! With
a sweep of his arm, snow and little dishes went off the parapet. He could not see, but he could hear the plops in the
water below. "That was seven at a blow all right," he
thought to himself, pleased. He dusted off his hands and
brushed off himself a little and then started sauntering
back. He let the snow fall on his upturned face and
watched between squinted lids how it fell on the empty
gardens. He really felt now as if he could stay out all night.
But he was not serious about it. He felt, too, that it would
be good fun to get into bed after doing the best act of his
life.

Hubert was not able to get into bed as soon as he had
planned. At the gate of the park, directly opposite Aunt
Charlotte's front door, he had to hide behind a tree trunk.
There in front of him was Fabian and the carriage, and
Aunt Charlotte herself was getting out of it. It hardly took
a wink of time for his feelings to change from being Sam-
son to being like the Babes in the Wood. After the door
closed and Fabian drove off, they were worse than that.
They were like someone lost in the Arctic. His feet were
cold, his mittens were wet and icy, snow was going down
his neck, and he could see as plain as day his frozen corpse
in the morning. They would be sorry for him, naturally,

but he knew he would be a great deal sorrier for himself. He stared at the house and got a little warmer from hope. Aunt Charlotte, having been let in by the watchman, was evidently going upstairs. The lights went out in the hall and on on the second landing. Then those went out, and after a year or two they winked from the third story. She had certainly gone into her room by now and closed the door, and Amlie would be with her, enclosed and far away. Hubert thought he might be saved. At any rate he would try the front door. If the night watchman hadn't noticed the lock was sprung, he would not have locked it again.

Having all this time been safe in emptiness, silence, and snow, Hubert found the trip back across the street full of danger. He had to wait for a policeman to go by and sidle round the tree to keep out of sight. He had to let a couple of carriages pass, and two men came along as slow as turtles. Behind all their backs he finally scuttered over and got up the steps and dared to try the door handle. It turned. He pushed and the door gave. Hallelujah. He was in the dark hall and could not see much right away, but he could see enough to get off his outdoor clothes and chuck them in the closet and then to feel his way to the bottom of the stairs. There, just as his foot was on the lowest step, a light hit him in the back and shone all round him. The night watchman had picked him up with his lantern.

"I just went out for a breath of air," said Hubert.

He kept on steadily. He didn't see what the night watchman could do to him. He was perfectly respectably going upstairs to bed in his pajamas.

CHAPTER SIX

It

The morning after the Horticultural Ball Theodore had the measles. It was bad, bad luck that this was discovered before they could all take the train to Summerton as they were supposed to do as soon as Aunt Charlotte released them. But he had woken up feeling so badly he had asked Hubert to take a look at him. Hubert's thoughtful opinion was that he looked like a boiled balloon. He even went to extremes, telling Theodore he better stay in bed.

"Not on your life," said Theodore, kicking off the bed clothes and wobbling to his feet.

Hubert went in to consult Jane. "He might have pneumonia, I suppose," he said. They thought about it worriedly.

"This would be a terrible place to let him have it in," said Jane consideringly.

"I thought of that too," said Hubert. "But almost anyone can notice there's something the matter with him."

Theodore did the best he could at breakfast to let them get away in peace by holding his handkerchief up to his nose.

"This blamed cold makes my eyes run," he said while Eliot and Amlie were bringing in food. His best efforts, however, made no impression on people who were natural busybodies. Before they had begun on toast and jam, a big gray woman who was Aunt Charlotte's masseuse came into the dining room and without saying "Good morning" or asking permission walked up to the back of Theodore's chair and looked behind his ears. Almost immediately they were all put into one of Bishop's cabs and sent back to Grandfather's. It was a hopeful sign that did not last long. From there they were not allowed to go any farther. Telegrams were sent back and forth as soon as Theodore was fussed upstairs by Nellie Flaherty, and it was decided that the Red House must not be "exposed."

So the whole Easter vacation would have to be spent in the city of Charlottesville. Moreover, Nellie Flaherty, scurrying and breathing hard through her nose, cleared Jane and Hubert out of the third floor and left them homeless in the hall while she got a room ready for Theodore's nurse. They found they had to reside in two little holes at the very back of the house on the floor below, and had to use Grandfather's bathroom.

"Not very convenient for us, I *must* say," said Hubert, "considering how long he spends in the bathroom."

"I like it," said Jane. "You can almost swim in the bathtub, and it smells of soap."

"That's just what I don't like; it makes my nose itch."

It was true; his convenience was not considered. No one's was, except Theodore's. It seemed a great deal of fuss for one little disease, they thought. They had all had diseases

now and then, except that Hubert had refused to catch the
mumps. Nurse had put him in bed with Edie and told him
to kiss her. This he would not do, but he had let her breathe
in his face and it had done no good. He had made up for
it when they all had "hooping cough." Hubert had
"hooped" all over everywhere, indoors and out, so that they
had had to be careful where they took him, and a great
many times he had had to eat two meals, one after the
other. Except for providing him willingly with extra food
he could not remember that his family had paid much
attention. Theodore, however, was wallowing in it. Grandfather's cook made him caramel custard by the gallon,
Miss Plunkett went up- and downstairs with drinks, and
Jane and Hubert themselves received nectarines and grapes
at the door sent by Aunt Charlotte. It worried Jane. If
grown-up people were so nice, there must be something the
matter.

"Maybe he's awfully sick," she said.

"Well, he's not dying," said Hubert firmly, "or the family'd be here to get his last words."

But Jane could not get over being suspicious.

Anyway they were not told, and they were not allowed
to see Ted. They tried. They were not certain they had
been near enough to the measles so as to get them before
school started again. But Miss Plunkett had stood outside
Theodore's door every time and said: "Your brother's resting just now." It seemed a very foolish thing to say about
Ted. They wondered if she had him tied down. But Plunk

had to have her own way, or she would "report." Hubert
knew all about her, as he had had to have her himself once
for swelling up with hornet stings.

"Who would she report to?" asked Jane. She hated the
mystery. "There's nobody here but us. Grandfather doesn't
like her."

They knew this because every morning when they joined
him on the landing, he would stand and tap his foot and
say loudly, "Where's that woman?" looking up toward the
third floor. He would not go down before Plunk came,
because he wanted to glare at her. And when she did come,
he did a lot of non-glaring at table. He would not look at
Plunk when he served her. If she asked for the butter, he
poked it over to her with one finger.

Meals were very uncomfortable. Everything was uncomfortable. What could they do when they had been in-
structed to be careful about breathing on anybody? By
Sunday they were terribly dejected. Theodore came out in
spots, but what was that? Nellie Flaherty announced it to
Grandfather when he came back from church.

"Has he indeed?" said Grandfather, hanging up his hat.
"Most intristing."

At dinner he picked up the salt and placed it unasked
in front of Plunk, and while he was peeling a pear, he
spoke to her. "Nellie tells me the boy is better."

"Much better, Mr. Cares, thank you," said Plunk briskly.

Grandfather did not say anything more, but he chomped
his pear down as if he enjoyed it.

Everyone in the house felt fine on account of Theo-

dore's spots except Jane and Hubert. They could not see
what difference they made. They probably made Ted look
more frightful, and he had looked frightful enough already.

On Monday morning a postal card came from Edie. It
was pretty good for Edie; they had not known she could
write one at all. It had a picture of five kittens in a basket—
that was pretty good too—and no stamp. Mary Bright had
to pay a cent for it at the door. Well, Edie couldn't know
everything all at once. Jane read it first and then showed
it to Hubert before it was sent up to Ted on one of his
trays. In the enormous crooked printing Edie was learning
at Miss Lincoln's, it said,

DEER TED
U BEDR COM HOM
THERS SOMTHING U R
NOT GOIN TO LIKE

No word came down from Theodore on his receiving
this news. Not a word was heard from anybody.

"It's like being left on a desert island," said Jane. "What's
the *matter?*" she wanted to know irritably at breakfast after
Grandfather had left the table. She could not help throwing a piece of roll at Hubert because he did not think seriously that Madam and Father were dead and no one would
break it to them. Naturally he threw the roll back, and it hit
her on the nose. There might have been further and worse
irritability but that Jane, while she was scrabbling on the
floor with her eyes watering trying to find the roll, saw in

her head a picture of Summerton. She stood up quickly wiping off the tears with her palms.

"Hubert! Do you remember the time we came to Charlottesville from Summerton by ourselves?"

"Sure," said Hubert carelessly. "What of it?"

"What's to keep us," said Jane impressively, "from taking the train to Summerton by ourselves and seeing what's the matter."

"Lots of things," said Hubert. "Besides what would be the good of that? We couldn't go home."

"We could get hold of Edie, though, and find out what she's talking about. We could find out if they're *alive.*"

Hubert thought it was all foolishness in the first place, and it took a long time to persuade him that they would not be found out and treated like people who had spread The Plague, in the second.

"If I remember rightly," said Hubert, "they put them in a black hole called Calcutta and smothered them to death." He was walking round the green parlor kicking furniture legs and wishing Jane would leave him alone.

But the more Jane talked the clearer *she* became that they could do it. It would be a cinch. Didn't Hubert realize that no one went to Summerton in the mornings? At least no one they knew. And no one they knew came back to Charlottesville in the afternoons. It was the other way round. Hubert tried to escape by saying he saw a cat in the backyard, but Jane made him sit on a green brocade sofa and listen. Didn't he realize they could waylay Edie somewhere?

"And be seen by everybody," said Hubert obstinately.

"We don't have to breathe on them," said Jane. She was sure they could manage it. They didn't need to get off at the Summerton station, where Mr. Haynes, the telegraph operator was; they could walk from Gray's, the little stop where the train got watered, and come round the back way by the Galway Road. "We did it before, the other way round," Jane persisted.

"We had our bicycles then," said Hubert sourly. "And it was summer."

"It won't do us any harm to walk," said Jane righteously. "We're getting awfully soft on these pavements."

"I'll go," said Hubert slowly, "but I wish I had a disguise."

Jane thought it a marvelous idea. Of course, they could both have disguises.

It took them two days to think of the proper thing and then ended in nothing better than somebody else's hats. Jane said she would borrow one from the fat girl up the block whom they had met in dancing school, and Hubert could borrow Martin's, Grandfather's outside man, when he left it on a kitchen chair while he took up the wood. Jane found that her new hope and energy showed her just what to do once Hubert was convinced. Summerton was under some dark spell, and she was going to get herself and her army, Hubert, ready to rescue it. She could think of anything and everything. Money she got out of Grandfather.

"Did you tell a lie?" asked Hubert suspiciously.

"No!" said Jane. "I said we wanted to buy a train."

"Glory," said Hubert. "He can't have much idea what things cost."

She knew how to get lunch out of Grandfather's cook and just what to say to Nellie Flaherty about a nice walk all over Charlottesville. She sent Hubert into the kitchen at just the right time to get Martin's cap. There had been just a little trouble over her own. The fat girl did not want to lend it without knowing where it was going and when it would come back. From the bottom of the steps Jane found this hard to explain. She said she and her brother were playing a game and the hat would be back that night. The fat girl thought perhaps she could play the game too and wear her own hat. Jane said simply and flatly: "NO."

"Take it," said the fat girl. "I don't really trust you *or* your brother, but take it. If I don't get it back, *my* brother'll come over."

Jane was sorry she had forced anyone to make such common threats. Why, you saw them in the funny papers! But she felt successful as she put on the hat in the hall in front of the mirror.

"Gee, Jane," said Hubert, awed. "You couldn't tell you from a weasel in that. It's great. It looks just like a griddle-cake."

"Put on your own," said Jane severely. When he had, she took a good long look at *him*. "The trouble with yours is," she said, "you can't see you at all. Come on."

The only scare they had getting to Summerton was at the Charlottesville station, where Hubert, peering out from

the earflaps of Martin's cap, said he saw Mrs. Penhallow
Gitlin, a friend of Aunt Charlotte's.

"Do you know her?" Jane asked, astonished.

"I spilt some tea on her once," said Hubert. "She might
know me."

But they did not think Mrs. Gitlin took the train to Summerton. And to make doubly sure of not meeting her, they
got on the car next to the engine. No one like a friend of
Aunt Charlotte's would sit up there on account of the soot.

Their real difficulty began on the walk from Gray's.
Before they had reached the middle of the Galway Road,
Hubert's galoshes had rubbed his heels raw.

"How *can* they?" said Jane. "You've got your boots inside."

"Easily," said Hubert. "They make the boots go up and
down."

It was quite a terrible journey up the Galway Road. The
ruts, half-frozen and half-muddy, made Hubert's boots
twist every which way. Also twice they had to turn off and
crash far into the leafless bushes on account of people who
came along. The first was Milldale Smith with his brown
Morgan picking her way daintily over the bad road, and
second was the Summerton swill chariot, whacking and
clattering, with William Swain letting his old white horse
tramp along the way he wanted. Jane, spying between the
tree trunks, loved to see them. She could hardly stay quiet
and let them go by. We *are* home, we *are* home, she kept
saying to herself. "Come on, come on, come on," she said
impatiently to Hubert. "We can't see the Red House till we

get to the corner." But her army was in bad condition. It was hobbling and saying "ouch" at almost every step.

"Take *off* your galoshes," Jane said finally, exasperated. "It was twelve o'clock at Gray's. If we take much longer, Edie'll be having lunch."

"Maybe she's in bed with a cold," said Hubert gloomily. "My feet are killing me."

They started out on the perilous stretch between the Galway Woods and the shelter of Uncle Warren's sunken lawn, one side of which bordered the main street. Jane could never have believed this stretch could be so barren. It was like Siberia. And suddenly something was the matter. Here they were in the middle of their own things, but it was dangerous. They were exiles. She started to run and tried to hurry Hubert, but as he was doing his best not to walk on his feet, he could only stumble along beside her.

"You're like an old horse with spavin," said Jane crossly, panting a little.

Just as they got to the edge of Uncle Warren's wall, another buggy turned into the Galway Road. They flopped themselves behind the wall and waited, with the cold of the slush coming up into their stomachs, until they heard it go by, and then crawled into the thicket of pines. There Hubert said he would take off, not his galoshes, but his boots. While he was doing it, Jane kept separating the pine needles and looking up toward the Red House. There was no one in that direction. She began to be afraid that even Edie might have gone away somewhere. She began to wonder whether they would see anyone ever again who be-

longed to them in Summerton. She was ready to be off the
moment Hubert got up.

"Where are you going?" he asked.

"Home," said Jane.

"In plain sight?"

The Red House in summer stood in a perfect bower of
shrubs and trees, and now for the first time Jane realized
that in early spring it had no protection at all. They had a
low-voiced conference that was almost a dispute. Hubert
wanted to go back. Jane would not do it. But she had to
listen to his arguments. What did they know about Edie
nowadays anyway, he said. What did she do in the afternoons? Maybe she grubbed in the house all day. Besides,
his feet were now freezing solid from the slush they were
standing in, his knees hurt from kneeling on rocks, his
head itched from Martin's cap, and he was hungry.

"You can eat when we get to the manure pit," said Jane
abstractedly. *That* at any rate had a sort of hedge of thick
brown stems where they could hide. But they had to get
across the main road and the Big Field first. There was just
one way to do it. Making Hubert bend double, she led him
through the culvert that went under the road and out the
other side. There they kept close to the wall and finally
were behind the hedge and under the barn.

"Now what?" said Hubert holding his nose. "This
place stinks."

Having got to the barn safely and chewed down a sandwich as fast as possible, Jane was now sure they could go
farther. Her idea was to skirt the carriage house at the

back, scoot past the dog yard, and dive into the Red House cellar. But she wondered if any general had ever had an army like Hubert. Even after she had given him more than his share of the lunch, he found things to object to. What was the point, he wanted to know every few minutes. Frankly, he said, he couldn't see it, and he was thirsty. He had never had such dry sandwiches since he was born. Besides the complaints, without his boots he squelched in his galoshes. You could hear him coming as if he were a traveling pump. Jane tried to quiet him down by looking at him hard.

"I can't help it," he said sheepishly. "They just do it."

In spite of it, getting to the cellar was no trouble at all. Pat was eating his dinner in the kitchen probably, and probably Cook and Gander were, as usual, listening to his inspiring conversation so attentively that they did not think of looking out the window. It was cold, damp, and moldy in the cellar, but here they were. Here they were at last in the Red House, in their own home. Hubert himself confessed that he was glad to see the familiar eyes of the wild black cat who always hid behind the furnace, and Jane felt so kind and thoughtful she wanted to pat him. She tried, but he ran away.

"Let him go," said Hubert understandingly. "He never did appreciate anything."

Jane led the way past the mushroom bed and through the furnace room and out into the large gray space under the Red House library. She stopped by the little steps that they had discovered last year came out through a trap door into the wood box in Father's study. Hubert at last saw, but he could not get over being gloomy too fast. "I bet the wood box is full of wood."

"Not this time of year," said Jane.

She was right. The trap door opened easily, and they were able to crawl into the great wooden chest behind Father's study chair. Their crawling covered their reefers with wood chips, but they did not care about that. They had somehow got into a watchtower, and now all they had to do was wait. Sometime Edie would walk down the corridor to the library, and they would hiss at her through the wood-box crack. First, however, they assured themselves that the top would lift. A crack of light came through as soon as Jane pushed upwards, and Hubert put a piece of wood in to hold it open. Everything was all right. There was a smell of leather and Father's cigars, so it was a little better than all right. They hunched themselves up with their arms around their knees and listened for a long time for footsteps. There were no sounds at all.

"When you think how they usually thunder round," said Hubert to his arms. Jane nodded.

Hubert fixed his galoshes a little more comfortably and gnawed his wrist while he listened.

"They must be eating themselves out of house and home," he could not help whispering after another long time. He took off Martin's cap and began jiggling it. "It's hot in here," he said, scratching his head all over.

"You might go to sleep," said Jane kindly.

"My bones are coming through," said Hubert, muffled.

He had put down his head on his knees again. "I'd like to have a conniption fit right here and now." But he did not move for another long time.

"I—think—I—hear—something," whispered Jane carefully, when they had been listening hard enough and long enough to hear to California.

"You mean that wheel-squeaking noise? So do I. If it's Edie, she needs her joints oiled."

The noise, a little louder, went up and down. "It's only the cat meowing," whispered Hubert, disappointed. "It's got in the furnace and is burning up."

"Can't you shush!" said Jane.

She moved over and put her ear to the crack. Something was certainly meowing.

"Golly," she said, "it *is* the cat. We better go and see. She can't be in the furnace. She's probably caught somewhere."

"If she is," said Hubert, not moving, "it'll be the very first time. Besides, this squeaking is in the house, not down cellar."

They listened until they felt as if their ears were stretching. Now the meowing was going up and down almost regularly. It was quite a ways off, but it was there, perfectly plainly. With their heads down, immovable, and hardly breathing, they concentrated on it.

Slowly, at exactly the same moment, they looked up and looked at each other. Hubert's eyes and mouth opened and his eyebrows went up almost to his hair. Jane grabbed his cap and stuffed it over his face.

"Don't say what it is!" she said in a ferocious whisper. "Don't you dare say it."

Hubert got the cap out of his way with a good whack at Jane's wrist. "Don't say it yourself. Let me go. I'm getting out of here."

"Hurry up!" said Jane. She tumbled him through the trap door and was just going to follow him when she turned back to pull the stick out of the wood-box crack. She let the lid come down with a bang.

"That's the stuff," said Hubert. He himself let go of the trap door while it was still wide open, and that went up with an even louder and harder bang. They seemed to have the same good ideas at the same time. Going past the furnace, Hubert stopped and opened its door. Neatly and quickly he rolled Martin's cap off his hand and onto the red and blue flames. Jane, behind him, tore off the fat girl's hat. "Wait!" she said, and the blue-velvet griddlecake landed on the flaming cap.

"The back way?" asked Hubert at the cellar door.

"No!" said Jane. "They don't deserve anything."

They were both beyond caring what would be thought. But they both wished that Hubert had his shoes on as they stepped into the carriage house drive and started down to the road. His squelching galoshes were not the right things to make anyone believe in seriousness. Pat did not believe in it, as he came out the kitchen door just as they were opposite and stopped to take a look at them.

" 'Tis the English Army to be sure," he said. He was

the most unrespectful and rude man it had ever been their pleasure to know, and they hated him.

They walked straight ahead while Pat took hold of his chin as if he were going to think, but they did not hurry, even when they knew that behind them he had turned back to the kitchen door.

"What do we care?" said Jane as they went round the horse chestnut at the end of the drive. Hubert understood her. Pat could tell on them. They could send everybody in the Red House shrieking and screaming after them. Without warning they had been practically made into orphans, and they did not see why they should care about anything.

Nobody did come after them as they walked with dignity under the bare maples that lined the sidewalk except Edie. They did not realize that she was there until they stopped at Uncle Warren's corner to pick up Hubert's boots. He would not put them on but tied the laces together and slung them round his neck. They climbed back over the wall deciding without a word to each other that they were not going to take the long walk back to Gray's but quite openly they would go to the Summerton station no matter how many germs they had on them. As they reached the road, they saw Edie on the other side, waiting.

"She knew it all the time, Jane," said Hubert. "Don't speak to her; she's a traitor."

But it was hard for Jane not to speak to Edie. Perhaps she wasn't a traitor, maybe she was just as much an orphan as they were. Jane took a step toward the road.

"Don't come near me," said Edie plainly.

"See," said Hubert. "What did I tell you?"

"Have you got the measles yet?" called Edie.

"We certainly have," said Hubert. "Phoooo. Come on, Jane, she's just come to gloat."

"I have not come to gloat," said Edie. She looked undecided and, Jane thought, a little small.

"What did you come for then?" she called back to be perfectly fair.

"I know where you were," said Edie, without answering the question. "You were in the wood box, weren't you? Did you hear IT?"

"Yes," said Jane sternly, "we did."

"Why don't you come home and do something then? I told Theodore to come home and *do* something."

"What would you suggest, bright eyes?" asked Hubert.

Edie tried to kick a stone out of the half-frozen ground. "You could give it the measles or some old thing like that."

"She wants us to murder it for her," said Hubert. "What do you know about that!"

"We won't do it," he said to Edie. "And don't you try it either. Do you want to get taken off by the Black Maria?"

"I thought that's what you came for," said Edie. She picked up the stone she had pried loose and aimed it at them, drawing back her arm. Jane and Hubert moved away. Edie was not much of a shot, they knew that, and the stone rattled across the road behind them. Seeing that she had not been able to make them pay attention, Edie herself moved away and went walking back to the Red House with her head in the air and her hands in her pockets. She did not look at all repentant.

"Of all things!" said Hubert. He could not get over having a female murderess in the family.

Jane felt thin and tired. The fury of having been made orphans was draining away, and in the station she hardly had energy enough to make Hubert put on his boots. He stopped lacing them up entirely when Mr. Haynes, the telegraph operator, came out of his office to watch and asked if they'd been up to see their little sister. As he was a friend, they had to answer him politely, but when he went back to his office, Hubert expressed himself.

"Another girl!" he said, almost growling. Jane did not know but what she agreed with him, but it made them both tireder than ever.

If they had known what to call it, they would have said they had lost their self-respect. Nobody asked them what they would like, nobody told them anything; they had no place to live but two cupboards at their Grandfather's, and now they knew there was another girl, probably like Edie. They did not like this at all because their worst feeling was about Edie. Somebody was going to have to see that she got straightened out. Sinking into the red plush seats and their own dismay on the warm, dirty train to Charlottesville, they went to sleep.

They were very cross when they woke up just before the Charlottesville station. They didn't want to get off and they didn't want to stay on, and they kept hitting each

other by accident with their elbows. It was not till they
got to the show window at L. P. Lappins that they were
sure there was not going to be a fight. L. P. Lappins was
the biggest grocery store in Charlottesville and it celebrated
everything. On Hallowe'en the whole store was done up
with pumpkins, goblins, witches, and orange paper; at
Christmas it smelled like a forest from the laurel and
ground pine; Valentine's Day it was strewn with hearts;
and though there was peace all over the world, L. P. Lappins got out its chocolate soldiers in March so that the
British could not capture Bunker Hill. Tonight it had an
American flag in the window. Jane and Hubert examined
it in every detail. The red and white stripes were sugared
almonds, the blue was candied violets, and the stars were
pieces of marshmallow. It had a short yellow pole made of
molasses chips. After staring at it a long, long time, Jane
said, as if she was talking in her sleep: "I would like to do
something awful right now."

"I would like to eat up the flag," said Hubert, not talking in his sleep at all. "Let's do it."

"No chink," said Jane, waking up.

"We'll charge it to Grandfather; good heavens, we ought
to have something for ourselves."

Jane thought he had said just the right thing.

They were particular to buy only the right kinds of
candy. It was inconvenient for the salesgirl. She had to
weigh the different kinds separately because they were all
different prices. "A silly way to have it," Hubert said. He
made her stick to it, and as he did not want to bankrupt

Grandfather, he only asked for a pound altogether. For some reason this made the salesgirl ruder still. "I should think they'd realize it's better than nothing," Hubert said in his lowest voice. "Aren't people always saying that every little bit helps? They don't seem to believe it, though, here."

It took such a long time that Jane turned her back on him in order to smell L. P. Lappins. She made a circuit of the middle counter and, on the way, bought a box of cracker sticks covered with chocolate. She could not get past them. Rows of lovely sticks neatly sleeping together. She breathed in way down to the bottom of her stomach. The smell of chocolate was good for being an orphan. When she came round to the candy again, Hubert was just ready. She showed him her box.

"Good work," he said. "Just the thing. I had her add a few peppermints at the end. I thought they'd be a good combination."

He also thought it would be nice to get a small box of cheese crackers and a bag of nuts. Since the ice was broken at L. P. Lappins, it seemed wise to put in supplies for a hard time ahead. They could keep them in the hall closet at Grandfather's and eat a little every day. Ted, they thought, might also like a change of diet by this time. But when they came out of Lappins' side door into the raw damp of the late afternoon, they felt hungry right then and there.

They ate the American flag and the cheese crackers and the chocolate sticks and the nuts sitting behind the fat stone woman across the way who was guarding the en-

trance to the Charlottesville library. Jane chose the place.
It was not very dry or warm, but she had always liked
the stone woman, who looked, she thought, like a good-
tempered cook. They had really meant to leave a little
something for Ted, but, once started, they could not stop.
They were very polite to each other. Jane offered her
things and Hubert offered his. "No thanks," they each said
together, "I'd rather have my own." It made them laugh
so much they had to put their hands over their mouths.
But after a while they swapped. Jane ate Hubert's recom-
mendation—a few candied violets on top of a cheese
cracker—and Hubert tried a chocolate stick with marsh-
mallows. No one disturbed them, and they finished everything, trying before they were through every sort of combination. They were left with four empty boxes.

"What if we do feel a little full," said Hubert, pulling his
reefer together with both hands.

He was reminded, though, of Peter Rabbit and how he
had gone in search of a little parsley, but he did not tell
Jane. He simply agreed with her that if they did not eat
again for a long time, all would be well. When it began to
drizzle, they thought they had better be going. They suspected it would be freezing pretty soon.

"Anyway, everything's empty," said Jane.

"What shall we do with the boxes? We can't take them
back."

Jane thought the stone woman could hold them in her
lap until morning, so they put them there, brushed off the
crumbs, and started away. As they went down the library

steps, they took a last look back to see if the boxes showed and stayed looking with one foot on a higher step. A small boy who had a cart behind him was standing on tiptoe and taking the boxes down. He was looking in each one and in each paper bag, putting his hand down inside to the bottom and feeling there. He could not seem to believe they were empty, because afterwards he tipped them upside down and shook them.

"He won't find anything" said Hubert.

"No," said Jane doubtfully. "What d'you think he wants?"

"He might want the American flag," said Hubert, "if he knew we had had it."

They could never decide why they thought it would be a good thing to follow the boy after he picked up the string to his cart and bumped it down the side steps of the library. They just did it. The boy saw them and walked backwards a little way, but he did not stop, and they did not stop. He took them down the Concourse for two blocks and then turned a corner. Round the corner he was waiting. It did not take very long before they were all in a back alley. It was an alley that did not seem very far from L. P. Lappins' or Grandfather's or any of the Charlottesville streets they knew, and it was just like any other alley, except they could not see the end of it. The end, instead of showing light, showed the darkness of an open door. The boy turned and looked at them once more and then went through the door with his cart. Jane stopped.

"Wait!" she said.

"No!" said Hubert.

She had to go with him right up to the door and look in. There was just a room. The boy was standing in it with his cart; there was a black stove against the wall, and there were four people on four chairs in front of it. Jane could not see one other thing in the room, and no one was speaking and no one was doing anything. The people turned their heads and looked at the door as she and Hubert stood there. And they waited. It was terribly impolite to be looking in at them, Jane felt, but she could not move. She had to wait too. It lasted until one of the people —a woman in a black dress—twisted her hands together and leaned forward.

"We're starving," she said.

The woman twisting her hands was the one that said this, but all the other people made a slight movement as if they were saying it too. The boy looked at them over his shoulder. Jane and Hubert had to move. They could not stay looking at people who were starving. It was a terrible thing to do, so they went away.

"Do you think they were faking?" Hubert asked about the middle of the block.

"It was a queer sort of room to be starving in," said Jane.

"Of all the silly remarks," said Hubert. "You don't have to starve in one kind of a room."

Jane could not follow what she had been trying to think about. She was listening to a sound behind them.

"That boy's coming after us," she said.

"Yup," said Hubert. "What shall we do?"

"We ought," he added, not waiting for her to answer, "to serve them a twelve-course dinner."

"Yes," said Jane, almost wildly. "Yes!"

"But how can we?" said Hubert.

It came to them how they could do it, or something like it, when they got back opposite L. P. Lappins and were looking at a window that was full of canned peas. They did not have to talk much about it. Jane was to stay out-side and keep track of the boy, who had rattled after them as they came out onto the Concourse. He was still behind them as they looked in the show window. Hubert was to go in and see what he could get. All they had to do then was put it in the boy's cart and go on home.

"Don't get peas anyway," said Jane. "I don't believe they have a can opener."

"I wouldn't," said Hubert. "They're terrible."

It was not hard keeping track of the boy. While Jane loitered by L. P. Lappins' door, he loitered up the street, looking in the gutter. When he found anything, the small-est piece of wood or old rag, he put it in his cart. And he was keeping track of Jane as well.

Hubert came out in quite a short time. And he did it with what Jane thought was a horrible fuss. Two man-agers, or whatever they were, opened the swinging doors for him and bowed him out as he carried a big white wrapped thing in both hands and on his stomach.

"Many thanks," he said to them as he went by. "My Grandfather's cab's just round the corner."

"I had to tell them Grandfather was having a party,

Jane, and sent me to get the food," he said breathlessly. "Have they gone? Gee, help, this is heavy."

He only had to hold it a minute longer, because the boy was there, right there, in front of them, and had moved his few sticks of wood to the side of the cart. Hubert put the enormous package neatly in. It showed like anything, much too much to take it up the Concourse, even though it was getting dark. But the boy fixed that. He took off a kind of jacket he wore and covered it up, and then he went up the gutter without a word. And Jane and Hubert turned toward Brand Street.

"What *was* it?" asked Jane. "Did you get anything decent?"

"Peasants in aspic," said Hubert.

"I thought that was some kind of people," said Jane slowly.

"Nope," said Hubert, "some kind of chicken. I saw it. It was awfully expensive, but there wasn't one other thing in plain sight to eat in that whole store."

The last thing they expected, after a slippery and exciting trip skidding to Grandfather's, was to find a fuss inside the front door. Remembering the peasants in aspic, they thought they had never had such a chance to be good in their lives, and they had taken it. But just the same, Nellie Flaherty was walking up and down the passage as if she couldn't stop, and it was on their account. As soon as she let them in, she raced back and forth, her hands clasped, and red in the face.

"Have *you* got the measles?" asked Hubert, feeling as if he was being witty.

Nellie did not answer. She stopped in front of them.

"Where have you wicked children been?" she asked. She did not wait to hear, but raced away again, pushing through the door to the pantry.

"Gee, I guess it's late," said Jane.

"I guess it is," said Hubert, chucking his coat on the floor of the closet hurriedly. "Look as innocent as you can."

They pulled themselves up the stairs by the banisters. They would have to let Grandfather see them and find out what he would do.

They might have known that as usual Grandfather would not do anything. He looked at them once over the top of his paper and then raised it again; only his foot went up and down faster than they were used to. They thought they had been dismissed, so they started to straggle out, stepping on each other in the narrow place by the fire.

"Halt!" said Grandfather suddenly. He was taking another look at them.

"You will apologize to Nellie to whom you have caused great annoyance." They waited on their toes where they had been halted. "And take yourselves to bed," he added. He raised his paper. "Begone," he said.

"We will," they answered eagerly.

They immediately did their best about Nellie, but they were not sure it was satisfactory. They had to say their apology through her keyhole because she had locked herself in her room and would not come out. But they kneeled

on the floor and spoke as clearly as they could. They had to
go away finally without any answer.

"She's not going to forgive us," said Jane.

Hubert did not care so much about forgiveness. If Nellie
had been in a good humor, he thought he might have persuaded her to get him some parsley, just as a precaution.
Instead he had to be consoled by knowing that they had
been sent supperless to bed on the only night he could
think of when he did not want to remember food.

They would have both been quite willing also not to
remember Theodore. They did not want to see him or have
any correspondence with him. If he knew what they had
heard in Summerton, in the Red House, he might have a
relapse, or do something else just as rash—get up and go
out in his stocking feet. That was what old Mr. McHenry
had done because of President Roosevelt, and he had gotten
pneumonia and died. Theodore's disapproval could be just
as bad.

Of course then it had to be just the evening when Plunk,
not knowing they had been punished, came down from
the third floor as soon as they had resigned themselves to
some interesting books—Hubert was even cooling off his
stomach a little by exposing it to the air in the privacy of
his own room—and said their brother was well enough to
see them if they would care to go up.

"I don't care to," said Hubert, when she came in to get
him. "But I might think about it if you'd get me a little
parsley."

He had to go without it. Plunk said to come now and

not be silly. She also looked behind his ears, although he took the pains to explain to her that that was the wrong place.

They cared about their visit even less when they got there. Ted was in bed leaning against some propped-up pillows, and he looked so white and clean it was embarrassing. Miss Plunkett had even washed most of his freckles away. They tried not to look at him, because he would certainly not want to be reminded of *that*. They sat on the opposite bed unable to get comfortable, and what was harder, not able to think of anything to say. Jane made a great effort.

"Do you feel better?" she asked politely.

But Theodore was not going to discuss his health. "I feel like thunder," he said. "Shut up about it." He took a postcard that Jane saw was Edie's off the table by his bed and skipped it down his blankets.

"What does she mean?" he asked.

Jane and Hubert stared at the picture of the cats in the basket. Now they had seen Ted, they felt more than ever that their news might kill him.

"Nothing much, I guess," said Jane.

"She never does mean much," said Hubert helpfully.

"Have you been home?" asked Theodore.

"We're in quarantine," said Hubert quickly. "We're not supposed to go anywhere."

"Have—you—been—to—Summerton?" asked Theodore. "I'm asking *you*," he said to Jane.

Jane nodded.

"What's up?"

Jane took a long breath. She didn't see any way out. If he was not told, it might easily be as bad as if he was. "They've got a baby out there," she said. "A girl."

Theodore turned his head away. "Didn't I tell you?" he said.

Jane and Hubert nodded. They had to admit it. A year and a half ago when he had mysteriously found out before anyone else that Father was getting a new wife, Ted had told them there would be a lot of squawky babies, and here one was, squawking like anything.

"What was it like?" Theodore asked calmly. It was hard for them to believe their ears.

They had to tell him they did not know. Ted put his head back and took a breath. What was the use of taking all that trouble for nothing, he wanted to know.

"It had an awful voice," said Hubert.

That was no news, and Theodore said so. "It may not be such a bad kid," he added surprisingly.

Jane looked at Hubert to see what he thought. She herself thought that Ted must be terribly weak from the measles. But Hubert was not thinking any more. He was holding onto his stomach. "I believe I better get out of here," he said to them formally, and then put both hands over his mouth and walked straight to Theodore's bathroom and closed the door.

"Let him go," said Theodore. "At the moment I'm interested in something else. We can train that kid ourselves, old lady."

Jane did not say that they had not had much luck training Edie. She was too much relieved. Theodore looked at the ceiling. "In my opinion," he said, *"she* ought to be allowed to have it. She has been very nice to us all, don't forget that."

"I haven't forgotten anything," said Jane instantly, sitting up straight. She hoped she would never be as blind as a boy. Why couldn't he see that that was just the trouble. Madam, who had been so nice to them all, was now going to have to be nice to that baby.

"Don't look so like a dying cow then," said Theodore. He took Edie's card and twirled it round his head giving thin war-whoops. "Hellcats," he said, "suffragettes, women's rights, votes for the bloomer brigade, rah, rah, rah."

Jane looked at her hands. "All right," she said slowly. "But if I were you, I'd tell Edie the same thing."

"I'll see to *her,* don't you fret," said Theodore.

CHAPTER SEVEN

Poor Widgy

When Edie came home from Miss Lincoln's one day at the end of April, instead of going into the house she sat down in the middle of the gravel road opposite the stone steps of the Red House and put her head down on her legging-covered knees. She was not disturbed for quite a while. Two buggies went by and turned out for her. Milldale Smith, who was next, peered down at her and then flicked her head lightly with the lash of his whip, but went on his way. It was not till Aunt Isobel came dashing along in her electric auto at ten miles an hour and turned whizzing into the circular drive to call on Madam that Pat got orders for Edie to be removed. He picked her up in just the position she was, planted her on the lawn, fixed her feet as if she were a dog in a show ring so that she would not fall over, and went back to the stables. There was no other sign from the Red House. Nurse did not even put her head out a window to say Edie would get appendicitis from cold damp stones. So Edie stayed where she was. Where was she to go, she would like to know? There was that baby that Madam had made filling up the front part of the house; there was Nurse and her very close veins at the

back; and there were Gander and Cook in the kitchen who
thought her too old now for loitering around there. Outdoors was no good either. Jane and Hubert were having
Theodore's measles at Grandfather's in Charlottesville,
Theodore himself had gone back to school, and what was
much worse than losing all her family at once, Edie had
lost Widgy. He had been gone for two weeks. Edie's head
sank lower. Ever since Christmas, day and night, she and
Widgy had been together. He was the most remarkable
dog in the world. He had saved them from dying of freezing to death in the Far North by chewing a footstool; he could
run like a greyhound after Old Bob, her horse; he would ride
on a tricycle or be pushed around in a doll's carriage. Some
things he might not have liked—wearing a bonnet for instance—but he was so remarkable that no matter what he
had to do, afterwards he put out his tongue and panted up
at Edie saying it was good fun. Even the day she had
discovered the ocean of violets on the far side of Grandfather's swamp—the light blue kind with petals like rabbits' ears—and been so overcome that she had had to lie
down in them, Widgy had stretched out at her side with
his face like hers on the petals. A dog must be pretty remarkable if he liked flowers. The other dogs she knew
would rather have nice fresh cow manure. But not Widgy.
She had brought as many violets home as she could carry
and scattered some at the bottom of her bed that night.
Widgy put his chin on them and went to sleep. He was
remarkable. But he was gone just the same. After the first
day Edie had gone around to all the farms on Old Bob and

asked if he had been seen. Everyone shook his head except
deaf Mr. Watkins, the cowman at the Hammonds'.

"Didn't know you had a dog," he said loudly because he
couldn't hear himself.

"He was a good dog," Edie shouted back.

"A coon dog?" said Mr. Watkins shaking his head.
"Them's the kind that wanders."

It was no use talking to *him*. Or anybody for that matter. They had ideas, but nobody knew for sure what had
happened to Widgy. Cook thought robbers, Pat thought he
might have been eaten by a fox, but after talking to Mr.
Watkins, Edie had an idea herself. There were heaps of
woodchuck holes in the meadows. Widgy liked woodchucks almost as much as he did violets.

"Do you *think*," she said to Father that night," that he's
stuck in a hole and can't get out?"

"He had quite a corporosity," said Father.

She knew what he meant. He sometimes talked about
her own fatness with that terrible word. She could see
Widgy joyously following the woodchuck into his hole.
And then, perhaps like that book called *Old Rough the
Miser* where a grumpy, disagreeable, mean muskrat keeps
some young squirrels shut up in his hole because he does
not like them, Widgy would be caught somewhere and
have to stay. Woodchucks certainly did not like him either.
Edie's idea grew and grew. She would have left the lawn
and gone in to change her now damp-seated leggings if
Aunt Isobel had not been coming out and thought of asking her to go for a ride in her electric auto.

"No, thank you," said Edie to her knees.

"What?" said Aunt Isobel, stomping her cane. "You're a mumbler. I can't hear."

"I said, 'No, thank you,'" said Edie louder.

Nobody would want to go in an auto with Aunt Isobel after the first time. Every poor old horse they had met had stood up on his hind legs at the sight of them. Edie had been horrified. But Aunt Isobel did not know this. *She* thought that the farmers should have better control of their animals. She turned back to Madam at the door.

"The child's clearly out of mind!" she said. After she had tried unsuccessfully to poke Edie's head up with her cane, she went away. And Madam went away. Back to that baby, Edie supposed. She did not stay much longer herself. Appendicitis was a big pain, and they had to cut you open to get it out.

"But I am *not* out of my mind," she said as she got up. Her wonderful mind had been able to think of a new way of looking for Widgy. Tomorrow was Saturday. She would start out in the morning and visit every woodchuck hole she could remember, put her head down it as far as she could get, and call to Widgy to come out.

Tomorrow was a lovely, lovely day, still and warm. But because it had rained a lot the first part of the week, you could hear the sound of water almost everywhere. It was the kind of day Widgy liked best. If he had only been there, Edie thought they could have had a good time going crazy together. Instead she planned her trip. No dogs. Bing and Sport made Widgy crawl on his stomach and look

cross-eyed with fear when they bounced around him. She
would not go on Old Bob because she always needed a
wall to mount again. But she took a good solid stick from
the woodpile in case she should meet a woodchuck face
to face. And she took provisions—a handful of Nabiscos
from the pantry closet while Gander was having her first
cup of morning tea. Then she took off her reefer, leggings,
and tam-o'-shanter, hid them under the piazza steps, and
was ready.

Suddenly she had to stand stock-still. Suddenly like a
thousand birds there was a burst of music from the gravel
road. Its shouting fell over her like a dish of ice cream. It
was the organ grinder and his monk! She couldn't miss it.
She was friends with both of them, but especially with the
monk. Edie put out one foot to run up the steps of the
porte-cochère, and then stopped. Widgy! But she would
stay hardly a minute with the monk. But Widgy might be
eaten in that minute. The tune was like laughing and running and standing on your head. She thought she would
simply have to listen for just another second. But Widgy
could be dead in that time. Edie turned and walked off
through the backyard, over Aunt Charlotte's lower wall
and lawn and past Grandfather's, and all the time the
monk's little delicate brown fingers were opening her own
to get the pennies inside. He was snatching off his hat at
her and putting it on. He was climbing the piazza roof to
look in a window and scare Nurse. And Edie was watching, squeezed together with love and laughter. Only she
wasn't really. She was climbing the hill to the Twenty

Acre Lot and supposing that if no one in the Red House gave Mr. Benedicta's monk any pennies, he might never come back.

"Where are you, bad dog, why don't you tell us?" she said aloud to Widgy, mad at him for a little while.

The first hole was not a success. It was a foxhole, as she could tell the minute she sniffed it, and she did not delay there, thinking that she might find some of Widgy's brown hair or his bones. Sedately she took the path into Aunt Charlotte's woods. Anemones were out; tree stems were red and purple; the sound of water was gone; but sweet, still smells, sun-baked smells, had taken its place. All she could hear were far-off cows and, nearer, chewinks in the underbrush.

There was a good hole, she thought, under an oak tree in the middle of Aunt Charlotte's domain. She would go there. But that one, she found, had become blocked with old oak leaves, and was no good at all.

"Widgy, Widgy, Widgy," she said to the woods around her. "You darn-it dog, why don't you come home?"

Where should she go now?

Putting her hands deep in her pinafore pockets and swishing her skirts, she climbed a hill out of the woods. At the top was Aunt Charlotte's hennery, and she knew of three burrows on the rough slope that ran down from the chicken yards to the woods. They were all open and she could get her head into each one. She called and whistled with more breath than whistle, into the earthy-smelling darkness, and then listened for a small bark or scrabble.

There was not a sound in any one of them. It was discouraging. She began to lose faith in her idea. She seemed to have walked for miles and miles, and she couldn't remember anywhere else to go. Just the same she was cautious going past the hennery. If she was seen by Mrs. Johnson, she would be told she was too far from home and would be sent back to the Red House with Aunt Charlotte's eggs. She took very small quick steps and kept her eyes on the grassy road. Mrs. Johnson did not see her, but Irene Johnson, who was playing with the cat on the side lawn, did, and Edie could feel her looking at her. She liked Irene. She was old but she was exceedingly respectful. Hubert said anyone with teeth that stuck out two yards would have to be respectful because there was nothing else left in life for them to be, but wherever it came from, Edie enjoyed it. And she did not mind at all Irene's being fourteen and nearly six feet tall. Edie looked up when she felt Irene dumping the cat and lolloping over to walk beside her.

"Good morning, Miss," Irene said, after trying to fit her steps to Edie's and not being very successful, no matter how many times she skipped with her feet. "You're off somewhere's I see."

At first Edie was not going to answer, but Irene's respectfulness seemed to make it necessary.

"I've lost my dog, did you know that?" she said.

"Not Widgy! Not that dear little handsome dog?"

Edie looked at her sideways, and Irene's face was as serious as her teeth would let it be.

"*You* didn't know him," said Edie.

"Everybody knows Widgy," said Irene simply. "I heard tell he was lost. Are you lookin' for him?"

"I'm calling in woodchuck holes," said Edie. "He might be down one."

They were almost at the end of the grassy road that came out on a wide path dividing Aunt Charlotte's domain in two. Edie could either go straight into the woods on the other side or swing to the right and come out in the high meadows above the Main Dairy, which overlooked all the west end.

"Wait half a minute, Miss. I know a good hole. I'll come with you aways and point it out." When they got to where the woods broke and you could see down into the half-moon valley, Irene pointed. "You see there," she said, "you go straight home—"

"No," said Edie. "I'm calling at woodchuck holes."

"Right there," said Irene, still pointing.

"That's Miss Hardy's orchard," said Edie, trying to see in a direct line with Irene's finger. "Nobody lets us go to Miss Hardy's."

Irene bit her knuckle with her awful teeth.

"You go straight home," she said, "and get your pa to help you. That's the best woodchuck hole in town. My ma works for Miss Hardy and she seen it."

Irene might know a lot about that woodchuck hole, but she did not know much about Father if she thought he was going to do any digging. Edie started off around the top of the half-moon meadows, eating up her Nabiscos as she went. Maybe, when nobody was looking, she could get

into Miss Hardy's from the back. Or maybe she could
crawl through the high grass like a snake and not be seen,
or perhaps she could come out at night. It took a long
time to get there, and once opposite Miss Hardy's wall it
was hard to give up the chance that Widgy might be over
there. Edie stood for some time jiggling herself and her
pinafore. She could see the hole was a good one—big, near
home, and a good pile of new clay piled at its entrance.
But she realized that she could see Miss Hardy too. She
was over by the stone wall that separated her property
from their own Big Field, and she was on her knees praying. She often did this, and Jane had once even seen her
in the rain. She *liked* to pray, and no children were supposed to disturb her while she was doing it. In fact, the
Cares children were not supposed to go anywhere near
Miss Hardy. It was a law of Father's that they were not to
set foot inside her wall. Edie thought about it. Trying to
rescue Widgy from a mad woodchuck was a good deal
different than running into somebody's yard just to steal
apples or make a noise. It was like being the fire depart-
ment, which was allowed to go everywhere to rescue
people no matter who was saying their prayers. She went
resolutely up to the wall and got over. She had to feel
where the hole was because she had to keep her eyes on
Miss Hardy's black back. It was nearer than she had
thought. Edie could see the upturned soles of Miss Hardy's
shoes as she slowly got down on her hands and knees to
call into the hole to Widgy.

"Come out of that hole, *you* dog," she said. "Widgy, I'm

at Miss Hardy's. Hurry." She stopped to listen. Did she
hear something? *Did* she? "Oh, Widgy, you ugly little
smutty-faced dog, come *out*."

This time she was so sure she heard something that she
did not look up to keep track of Miss Hardy. Her head was
as far down the hole as she could get it when her wrist,
lying out behind her, was seized and held by some bony
fingers, fingers like Theodore's, just like iron.

"Child," said Miss Hardy, pulling her and shaking her
as Edie scrambled, "you have offended the Lord."

"What?" said Edie, straining back. She did not like
being looked at by Miss Hardy. Her eyes were like black
ink. "Let me go," she said, whacking at Miss Hardy's hand.
"I'll tell my father."

"You must repent—repent—repent," said Miss Hardy. "I
have been praying for your father."

She moved across the orchard grass, and somehow, unless
she fell flat down, Edie had to move with her.

"I won't come," said Edie, trying to stick in her useless
sneaker heels. "I was only looking for my dog." She tried
to step on Miss Hardy's feet, but the long black skirts were
in the way and she stumbled.

"Up, child, up," said Miss Hardy, jerking her to her feet.
"The noontide waiteth, and you are a miserable sinner."

Miss Hardy was a terribly strong old lady, and Edie
began to be more than a little afraid of her lighted eyes;
she began to be afraid of everything that was happening,
so afraid that, although she thought of biting Miss Hardy's

hand, she felt she better not do it. She squeezed down at her side instead, trying to disappear.

Miss Hardy led Edie, humping and twisting, into her unused barn, opened one of the old box-stalls with high iron-grills, and swung her into it.

"Pray," she said. "Pray with all your strength, or there will be weeping and gnashing of teeth. I will pray with you."

She closed the heavy box door and was just going to slip the bolt across when Edie, from the inside, gave the door a hard, frantic push. It pushed Miss Hardy away a little for a second, and in that second Edie was out through the crack and free. She ran like a rabbit. Hubert would have said he didn't know she could get such a move on. She didn't go over the wall in the right place. She dashed at it anywhere and dashed into a lot of hard stems. She went through them headlong, but her foot caught on the tumbled wall beyond them and down she went on the other side. Safe, but a terrific belly flopper on the hard ground. It knocked her wind out, and she had to roll over on her back and look at the sky while she gasped in little breaths to get it back. A lot of tears came out of her eyes and rolled into the grass. "O-O-Oh, I'm dead," she thought, and was so sorry the tears came faster. Then it was all right. She could breathe right down to the bottom of her stomach again. She lay a minute doing this just for the fun of it, but very soon the fun was over. She remembered Widgy. He was still inside Miss Hardy's wall. She was almost sure she had heard something inside the wood-chuck hole. He was there with nobody to help him, and she was not going to dare go back to try to rescue him. Big, hot tears made little streams on her cheeks. While they were doing this, there was a tiny touch on Edie's face where the tears had made it wet. "Get away, bug," she said aloud, and brushed her cheek. But the bug came back and fluttered at her face again. Edie sat up brushing her face thoroughly and looking to see what was teasing her.

Her eyes opened wide. It was a little dog, a terrible-look-ing little dog with sunken eyes and a grinning face, noth-ing but hair and bones, and he could hardly stand up. He rocked on his legs, and then tried to sit down and fell over. It was Widgy! He scared Edie. She didn't know what to do with him. She didn't know what was the matter. She got down on the grass and put her face close to his. "Widgy," she whispered, "little dog, are you sick?" Widgy staggered to his feet and tried to lick her wet face. The more tears that ran down, the more he tried to get at them. Edie thought it was love, but she hardly dared to touch him, he looked so breakable. She let him lick as hard as he wanted. She would have liked to lick him back, but he stopped when the tears stopped, sat panting and looking at her with his sunken eyes, and then fell over. Edie thought she would go crazy because he was going to die and she didn't know how to stop him.

Afterwards the others called her names. "Don't you real-ize you can't be down a woodchuck hole for two weeks without starving?" said Hubert. Theodore thought she was a first-class moron. And Jane said she must say it wasn't very bright behavior. Edie wished she hadn't told them. They had not been there; they did not know that the way Widgy looked had knocked every thought out of her except that he was sick and she must get him home.

When Edie had picked Widgy up, she began to cry again. He was so thin he felt like sticks. The sticks struggled in her arms to get to her tears. "Yes, little dog," she said, "yes, yes, yes." Going over the sunken brook, Widgy almost tried to kill himself to get away. "Quiet, little dog, quiet," said Edie. "You'll hurt yourself some more." It was a dreadful thing that he could not know she was going to help him. "What *is* the matter, little dog?"

Suddenly it began to rain, a regular small April shower that fell down without warning and with big infrequent drops, and Widgy sat up and snapped at them. Then Edie at last saw what the trouble was. She had to think a minute what to do. It didn't seem the right thing to put Widgy into such a lot of cold water as there was in the brook, so she set him on the bridge, where he at once began wobbling back and forth looking down at the water. Edie got into the brook herself and, cupping her hands, held them up to him. Her fingers leaked, so that Widgy did not get much at a time, but there were enough times, so that Edie thought he could live to get home where she would give him a big bowl of milk and an enormous steak dinner. All the way home with her dog held carefully in her pinafore she thought of the delicious things she would find for him to eat.

It was lucky for Edie and Widgy that she went into the barn to let him have a good lap out of the watering trough before she gave him his feast. Pat was there cleaning bridles.

"Is it yourself?" he said. "I was just thinking could you be et by one of them little bastes."

"I found Widgy," said Edie proudly.

"Did you now?" said Pat, turning. He looked at the poor ball in Edie's apron and dropped the bridle, which swung back and forth on its hook till he absent-mindedly stopped it with his hand.

"The little lad don't look himself," he said.

"No," said Edie. "He's thirsty and starving. I'm just going to give him a drink and a feast."

Pat picked Widgy out of Edie's apron with one great hand and held him up.

"He's pretty sick, isn't he?" said Edie fearfully. She could see Widgy trembling all over.

Pat did not answer immediately. He held Widgy to his shoulder and squatted down so that he was face to face with Edie.

"Miss Edith," he said, "will you let me handle this now, will you truly?"

"I was only going to give him a feast," said Edie sorrowfully, "because he's starved."

"Go you into the kitchen then," said Pat, "and get that cook there to give you some warm milk. Just a little, mind, while I make a bed for the poor lad. His digestion's in bits and shtrands."

Edie was let off lunch, or at least she did not have to come to the table. When she appeared in the kitchen, Gander flew out of it to report to her stepmother, and Madam came to look at her and so did Nurse.

"Sure, we thought the cows had you, Miss," Gander said.

Edie flung herself at her stepmother. "I want some milk," she said. "I just want some warm milk. Make them get it for me." She tried to explain Pat's orders and Widgy's adventure.

Madam did not interfere when Edie took out the milk herself or while she was sitting by Widgy where he was lying on a nice blanket Pat had found for him. She only made Gander bring out a sandwich.

"Take it away," said Edie.

"Eat it now, Miss," said Gander. "It'll keep up your strength."

"Take it away, I said," said Edie. And when Gander still stood there, she swept the sandwich off its plate and onto the barn floor.

"Shame on you now," said Gander, "behaving like a monkey."

Edie did not care how she behaved. She was not going to eat while Widgy was starving. She sat beside him all afternoon feeding him the way Pat showed her, first water and then milk, six laps at a time, with a long time between.

"*Why* do I have to do it this way? I don't want to," she asked Pat while she was waiting and waiting on the floor of the harness room. "I want to give him something *good.*"

"I don't know, Miss, 'tis the way it is," said Pat. "No crayture can stand more than a scrap of food after starvation."

"Suppose you *do* do it," said Edie.

" 'Tis the death of them to be sure," said Pat.

It took Edie a long time to go to sleep that night. She shivered herself for a long time, thinking how nearly she had been the death of Widgy. She had to remind herself many times that when she left the barn, Widgy was asleep, and Pat had promised to give him more milk in the middle of the night.

In the morning Edie dressed fast to get back to the barn. As she came down the steps of the porte-cochère, there was her little dog himself on his four feet in the barn door looking toward her. Edie got down on her knees in the driveway. "Widgy, here boy," she said. "Here, here, little boy." And the minute he heard her voice he came.

Pat came to the barn door wiping his hands on a rubbing cloth.

"He's as full of water as a tank," he said. "When you've had your own breakfast, I belave he'd fancy some oatmeal."

But Edie did not wait for that. She put a teaspoonful of porridge in her own bowl with a few grains of sugar and a little milk and brought out Widgy's feast.

"I'm not being stingy," she said to his ear at the edge of the bowl. "I'm just getting you over starvation."

Widgy looked at her and then walked slowly back to his blanket and lay down with his head on his paws to wait for the next meal. *"He* knows he's going to get it," said Edie, nodding to Pat.

"Sure thing," said Pat. "You done well."

Edie put her arms tight around her own shoulders. "I love myself," she said, going across the yard to her own meal. "Oh, I just love myself."

CHAPTER EIGHT

The Marvelous Kid

For the moment Theodore thought that life was worth living. He was at home again at last; he was at the Summerton Fair; it was a good day in June; it was in the middle of the class for jumpers; and it was just at the moment when Willy McHenry's chestnut hunter sat down on her tail at the first jump and knocked it to bits. Willy had not gone off, that would have been too much to expect, but Theodore did not object to small consolations just now. He was lying on his stomach beside the stone wall that bordered one side of the meadow behind the Summerton church, chewing grass blades, and able at last to squirm with a little pleasure. It was about time. It had been a perfectly awful spring. There had been his measles, Jane and Hubert's measles, Aunt Charlotte's account of the Horticultural Ball (greatly exaggerated), school reports, meeting Madam's baby! The younger kids had been on the verge of behaving like such loons that he had taken a good deal of pains about Madam's baby. In vain. The most enlightened must acknowledge that it was cross-eyed and perhaps feeble-minded. Hubert had named it The Fair Christine because it was anything but. That had leaked out. At least it had leaked as far as Nurse, who had gone weak in the upper story about the baby. Last but not least, Edie had got herself into such disgrace that she was not allowed to ride in the Fair. The last time she had been taken to church she had rubbed shoe polish along the foreheads of the Lamphrey boys who were kneeling in the pew behind.

Theodore spat out his grass blade and chose another. He supposed that perhaps Father had a right to be a little annoyed. But if so, why was he deliberately planning more trouble for himself, and for them? While they had been innocently getting their tack together to saddle up and go up to the fairgrounds, they had been summoned by Madam to the Rose Parlor, and there, Serafine Holland—a ten-year-old cousin they hardly knew—had been sprung on them.

"TODAY?" Theodore had asked rather wildly.

Their stepmother thought they could spare enough time to meet the four o'clock train. Pat would take them down to the station and then home for tea. They could go back to the Fair for the balloon ascension.

"She's a scrawny female with hair. That's all I can tell you," he had said on the way back to the tack room. "Would you kindly take your forms out of my way and go and do something on your own account?" This they would not do quickly enough, so that he had had to brush the forms of his brother and sisters aside and, after squeezing a sponge slightly into Jane's hair, had made a dash for freedom with his tack over his arm.

Now, as Theodore watched Boney McHenry take her turn over the jumps on her even bonier polo pony and do

so well that Cinder did not stand a chance, his pleasure
was marred. It was just another example of the trouble a
person was always having with women. Boney's old bag of
bones could not possibly make a mistake, and Boney got
the credit. As the crowd clapped, he got up and went over
to sit down on the step of Grandfather's beech wagon to
watch the stone-hauling. Father had put in Harry Houdini to make up more contests; no one knew why. When
Harry refused to pull at all and Grandfather said: "I believe I recognize one of your family," Ted was disgusted.
The crowd roared, and Grandfather told Cochran he
wished to go. Theodore had to get up quickly and find
another seat. He visited the Antiques and Horribles Band
and stood beside them while Barney Moon conducted
them in "The Wearing of the Green." He visited Aunt Isobel in her electric auto, where she had crazy Miss Hardy
shut up, and heard that they were talking about satin for
coffins, and he stood with Father, who was looking in cattle
pens and smoking cigars with the farmers. In spite of females, he suddenly realized, as a little breeze brought the
smells of young cows, grass, and wild roses, that he was in
Summerton. That he was back. That he was here again,
safe. Besides, it was amazing how nothing ever seemed to
happen except in Summerton.

Father, of course, had to shatter this feeling.

"As soon as Pat gets harnessed up, it's time for you kids
to be off," he said.

When Theodore passed Madam where she was sitting in

the runabout holding May and June, the stout little cobs, he could hardly smile, although he wanted to, because she looked wonderful in her big hat. He joined the kids, who were sitting on the grass with their hands round their knees discussing obliviously the balloon ascension. He gave each of them a slight poke with his boot.

"Get a move on," he said. "We are now about to welcome another vampire to our midst."

Theodore's scrawny female and vampire turned out to be a medium-sized girl with straw-colored hair cut short and brushed forward. "Oh," thought Jane enviously. Her conformation was wonderful—long slim legs, neat quarters, good shoulders, big mouth, and eyes wide apart—and they could not complain about her clothes. She wore a dark blue suit and a round hat on the back of her head. Beside her on the car steps were a tall pair of riding boots and a large green bird cage, which had a black bird in it.

"Heaven preserve us," said Theodore. "She's brought a zoo."

But Jane and Hubert and Edie could not laugh. This was an entirely different sort of female than they had been led to expect, and they needed time to rearrange their insides.

Serafine did not bother them while they were doing it. She shook hands with each of them in a manly way and got herself and her bird into the front seat without help. All the way back to the Red House she talked in a low, experienced way to Pat about horses. The Cares could hear her, but clearly only once. That was when she asked Pat courteously about the racing speed of Harry Houdini.

"Begorra, Miss," Pat said loudly. "He could trot all day in the shade of a tree."

Serafine turned and gave one swift glance at the seat behind her, smiling slightly.

Father and Madam had gone home before them and were waiting on the porch. "Hello, Uncle John, hello, Aunt Elsie," said Serafine. "Glad to see you after all these years. Thanks for asking me," she said. "I hope you don't mind a bird that's come with me. He's easy to feed. He only eats raw meat."

"I hope he won't get a look at The Fair Christine," said Hubert so only Jane could hear him.

Serafine settled down on the edge of a piazza chair near the tea table and ate everything that was offered her. If Madam or Father asked her a question, she took an enormous swallow and then answered. But as soon as nearly all the toast and cake were gone, she conversed with Father of her own free will.

"I hear you've got some fine horses round here, Uncle John."

"You have been talking, I perceive," said Father, "to that master romancer, Mr. Mullen."

"There's one called Black Night, isn't there?"

"That's my horse," said Father, stirring his tea.

Serafine ducked her head. "I could ride him, I bet," she said.

"No one rides him but Father," said Jane quickly. "He's dangerous."

"You'd fall off," said Edie.

Hubert got so excited he kicked the table leg by mistake and made all the cups rattle.

"How much do you bet, Uncle John?" said Serafine. "Put up or shut up."

Theodore, who was sitting on the porch railing, reached up and held onto the gutter. But Father only leaned forward and took a cracker.

"How is your father?" he asked.

"You mean Wolf?" asked Serafine. "Wolf's fine. That's what we call him," she explained. "Well, sometimes he's fine, Uncle John." She muffled a small explosion. "And sometimes he's black and wild. You know my father," she said.

"And the rest of the family?"

"We're all fine. That is, you knew Mother was in bed, didn't you? Having a baby? I guess that's why I'm here. Did you know," she said, turning to everybody, "that a baby is the ugliest and most helpless creature born into the animal world? No fur, no claws, no teeth. Just a lot of bare skin?"

There was quite a silence. Hubert picked up the plate with the last piece of cake. "Have some?" he said.

"Sure," said Serafine, but before she took it, she asked: "Will anybody else?" And got up and offered the plate to everyone in the circle.

When Jane and Hubert came downstairs again after

showing Serafine her room, they found Theodore walking round and round the backyard slapping his leg. They both stood and stared at him.

"What's the matter with him?" Hubert asked. "Do you think he's got St. Vitus's dance?"

"Maybe he's slapping mosquitoes," said Jane with her hands in her pockets.

"Well, if you ask me, I doubt it," said Hubert thoughtfully.

The next morning the Cares found themselves taking care of Serafine's black bird Consuelo. They were scattered in all directions. Jane was pumping up the village hill on the way to get raw meat, Hubert was arranging a bathtub with a flower-pot saucer, Edie was crawling through Grandfather's asparagus for chickweed, and Serafine herself was cleaning the big cage. Theodore was taking Consuelo to walk on the end of a string. When the others came back from their errands, they lay down to cool their stomachs on the sand pile.

"Will someone kindly tell me what we are doing this for?" Hubert asked, when Serafine had gone for the hose.

"To be agreeable, Fatso," said Theodore, as he lunged Consuelo a bit to make the exercise better. "You've heard of it, I daresay."

Hubert blew a hole in the sand pile to have room for his breath.

"What do you know," he said to Jane softly into the hole. "The Terrible Tempered Mr. Bangs himself!"

From then on there were other things that surprised

them about Mr. Bangs. He was polite while he was playing croquet, even after he had been hit into the shrubs, and on Uncle Warren's new tennis court, instead of throwing his racquet at the backnets and pawing up the court like a stallion and trying to hit everyone in sight with balls when a shot went past him, he just beat himself on the knee a little.

And there was the night of the thunderstorm!

This was a thunderstorm that became famous. It concentrated right on Summerton and seemed to be splitting it in pieces. Father and Madam were in Maine for a few days, so the servants came up and sat in the boys' room and said their prayers—calling to God and His Mother to save them. Nobody could pretend they weren't scared. Jane hoped she would die—quick—before she had to be any more scared than she was. Hubert and Edie got under the bed and said they were pigs so that they could squeal and make a lot of noise. Serafine sat between Cook and Gander, where somehow she had been captured, until Ted beckoned to her with his head. Then she leaped away and sat beside him, cross-legged, with her head down. When a big crack came, the flash and the bang seemed to lift her to her feet.

"My bird!" she had said hoarsely. "He's alone."

The thunder and lightning were so loud and constant it was hard to tell what she said. But she began to step over Ted's feet.

"I must get him," she said. "My bird!" she said into Theodore's face.

Nurse, in a rocking chair, heard her between the rosaries she was saying over The Fair Christine. There was just enough lull for her to be heard too. "No need to be thinking of vermin, when there's mortals in danger," she said and went immediately on with her Hail Marys.

Serafine hopped over her legs. "My poor bird, he's alone," she said loudly to Nurse. She waited for another roll of thunder to pass. "He might die of fright, you know."

Nurse had gotten up and barred her way to the door. "Stay where you are, Miss," she said. "The bird cage is of metal. I'll not have it brought here. Hail, Mary, Mother of God, Save Us," she muttered quickly, bending over The Fair Christine, as the whole room shone from a flash. Serafine had dodged in the following darkness and was out the door before Nurse could do more. But Nurse waited for her to come back. Theodore had pushed himself to his feet. "Sit down," he said to Nurse. As the thunder carried his words away, he had to say it again. "I said sit down," he yelled. "There!" he said, pointing to the rocker. Serafine came back, taking, for some reason, high tiptoe steps, holding Consuelo as far from Nurse as possible. She took her place just as she had been, beside Theodore, with the cage between her crossed feet. When the worst crack of all came, so that they thought the Red House must be split in half, she looked up at Ted. He managed to swallow his Adam's apple and shake his head. Jane could just remember through the glare of her fright that Nurse kept saying "vermin" and that Serafine shrank into a still, still figure leaning against Ted's shoulder. And she could remember that Mr. Bangs, even when the storm got better, did not ask Serafine what the devil she thought she was doing.

They all came out alive. The Red House was not touched. They could not even find a damaged tree the next morning. Only a paper plume, which Edie had got at the Fair and left out to get some night air, was gone forever, and Serafine, everybody knew for sure, had made an enemy. Nurse would never get over her endangering The Fair Christine with a metal bird cage.

Whatever made her do something still worse after this, the others would never know. The Cares had all had to go to Charlottesville with Madam when she got back from Maine to get summer clothes, and when they came home, Nurse and Serafine were both in the front hall standing side by side, waiting. Nurse was shaking and Serafine, although she was not wet, looked as if she had been drowned. They saw at once that they must move away and let their stepmother settle whatever it was, but they were not gone before they heard that Nurse was giving notice that instant minute because Serafine had moved the baby carriage away from the maple tree and into the laundry yard.

"There's gypsies about, Ma'am," they heard Nurse say. "How was I to be knowing?"

"It wasn't a very long way, Aunt Elsie," said Serafine.

They heard her come slowly upstairs, and when they met her on the way down to dinner, she faced them apologetically. "I said I was sorry," she told them, "but I don't think the old lady likes me, just the same."

It became an accepted thing that Serafine had better stay

out of Nurse's way. It wasn't hard, because Nurse had almost nothing to do with the children now. She had graduated to The Fair Christine as soon as Edie could be persuaded to brush her own hair and change her socks. But it was not very pleasant, as Theodore said, never to know when you came round a corner whether you might meet the Old Harry herself. Still, no one was thinking of Nurse when the great excitement occurred.

Madam lost her diamond sunburst. Of all the wonderful things she had done for them, the Cares thought for the first few days that nothing was quite as good as this. And she couldn't have made the mystery better if she had tried. She hadn't been anywhere where she had worn it and she hadn't done anything that would have made her take it out of her jewel box. She had been looking for something else and noticed that it had disappeared. Father suggested that it was at the jewelers being cleaned. Gander asked could a rat have taken it off? Nurse inquired as to whether the children had been tampering with things? Cook turned out the kitchen cupboard and wanted to know could she have dropped it in the flour barrel? Pat brushed out every carriage and said did she remember to have had it to drive with her? Madam said "No" to them all. Her face was anxious, and she looked anxiously at other faces.

"We've got to find it," Jane said to the others. "It belonged to her dead mother."

No one objected to trying to find it. Theodore as Sherlock Holmes and Hubert as Dr. Watson, with their three faithful officers from Scotland Yard, went over the Red House on their hands and knees.

"You don't suppose The Fair Christine ate it herself?" Theodore asked, when they could find nothing.

When, on the third day after it was missing, Madam offered a twenty-dollar reward, Sherlock Holmes, Dr. Watson, and the officers looked in places where even they did not think it could be.

"Suppose someone else found it?" said Hubert. "Twenty dollars! It would support me in luxury for the rest of my life."

"Well, you won't get it, old boy," said Theodore, coming out of the library chimney and bringing quite a good deal of soot with him. "Five into twenty is just four dollars, but I don't suppose you learned that where you went to school."

Hubert, after the others had gone to bed, tried to get up and look a little on his own account, but Ted heard him and kept his knee on his stomach until he gave in.

The morning after this, Serafine was late to breakfast. Not much. Just enough to come into the dining room alone. As she passed Father's place, she raised her left hand to the edge of the table and tipped it open beside his plate. The diamond sunburst slid off it with a little bang, and she walked on to her chair. Father looked at it and at her without a smile.

"How did you come by this, Serafine?" he said.

Serafine first sat on her hands, then rubbed her face, and then put her hands under her again while Father waited.

Finally she became quiet and looked at him with a kind of grin.

"I dreamed where it was and went and found it," she said.

"Rubbish," said Father.

He closed his paper and, while Gander was changing one plate for another, looked over their heads to the far windows. He did not speak again for all the rest of breakfast, and Serafine did not seem able to say a thing either. The sunburst that had been found in a dream lay there looking at them all.

If anyone thought that later the mystery would be unraveled, they were, as Hubert said, "gravely mistaken." Grave was just the word for it, and gloom, he thought, would have been still better. In fact, for a while his own home was the worst place to live in that he could think of. Serafine would not tell where she had found the sunburst, and when she was asked how she found it, she said over and over again that she had dreamed where it was. Father, after his first words, asked no more questions. He and Madam looked at Serafine wonderingly a great many times, and it was easy to see that there was some hesitation in Madam's hand when she gave her the twenty dollars, but they were going to take her word. Jane and Hubert and Edie decided, sitting in the cool of the mushroom bed, that this was what they would do too. But Theodore was not at this conference. He refused to come. This was because Serafine's story about a dream had made him realize that no matter how hard a man tried he could never be friends with a woman for long. He did not believe in dreams. And he did not believe in telling lies. In a flash he was almost fatally disillusioned. And he did not mind stating his opinion frankly. It was that Serafine had turned out to be an awful sneak.

"Why won't she tell where she found it, tell me that," he kept on saying wherever he was. "She may have hidden it somewhere herself for all we know, to get the credit."

This made him feel really as if he was going to choke to death. Here was this kid telling lies in order to be famous. He told Jane she ought to try to save her.

"How?" Jane asked.

"Tell her it's not honorable to be a sneak," he said.

Jane wouldn't do it. "She's not the kind of person who tells lies," she said.

Theodore thought that probably she didn't know any better. He was ashamed to look at her any more. It scared him to think what would happen to her later in life. And there was another thing. He discovered she was obstinate and hard. When he tried to save her himself, she would not do what he wanted. She sat with her head hanging down just like an old southern mule and would not answer.

This was why he got the carriage whip one afternoon and took it out to the circular drive where Serafine was still standing. He had had an argument with her finally. She had answered him back. But as he knew he was right, he wasn't going to listen to her arguments. He was going to make her come round.

Theodore, after he had put the carriage whip back in

the socket of the democrat wagon, went out to the back of
the rubbish shed to smoke a cigarette. He had to do it. It
had been forbidden by Father on pain of being sent away
from Summerton, on pain of having to go to a camp for
months, on pain of death almost, but he had to do it. This
final trouble that he was in about women was the worst of
his life. He couldn't make it out. All he wanted to do was
help a seemingly nice kid. Gosh, he had liked her. And
all she would do was tell lies. He had just touched up her
legs a bit with the whip to make her see where she was
wrong, and she had insulted him a dozen times. As he got
out his cigarettes and matches, he noticed his hands were
shaking and had to wait a minute before he lighted up. He
leaned back against the sun-warmed boards of the wood-
shed after his first puff and blew out a long, hard stream of
smoke. That made him feel better.

Theodore was only allowed to feel better for about three
good puffs. After this, that cigarette was the worst he was
ever to smoke—before, then, and for the rest of his life. He
had just relaxed with the sun comforting him. He was
thinking that perhaps he could go to sleep and forget his
troubles when he heard a noise in the lane by the manure
pit, and there was Serafine. What in the world *for?* She
did not see him at first because she was rubbing her wet
face so hard, but he did not have time to blow the smoke
away before she stopped and stared. She looked her fill and
then turned and walked back. Being a girl, who could tell
what she would do? One thing was exceedingly likely. She

would certainly be influenced by the carriage whip. Theodore groaned. Good-by to vacation, good-by to everything
decent in the world. He threw his cigarette under the privet
hedge, ate a couple of jujubes, although that would make
no difference now, and walked away. He walked with his
hands in his pockets and head forward as if he were deter-
mined to go a long way.

The Red House was always very silent after the Cares
children had gone to bed at night. Summer sounds came
in every window, but in the house itself the smallest crack
or creak could be heard. Father and Madam's voices became plain at night, not words, but their separate low
sounds. The kitchen was silent with just a murmur from
the laundry, where Cook, Gander, and sometimes Nurse
sat to try to get a draft; the dining room was dark and still;
the hall outside Edie's door where the lamp burned was
quiet except when the curtain made a little slap from the
wind.

That night the quiet was broken suddenly and hurriedly.
Jane, who was not quite asleep, heard a man's voice in the
front hall. It was only Father coming in from the porch, she
thought. No! For some reason she had to turn on her back
and listen again. It was Pat's voice, talking fast. Why?
What for? What happened next she hardly had time to
hear. There was a stir in the hall as if many people were
there. Gander's voice said something, and Madam's and
then Father's. When Jane reached the head of the stairs to

find out what was the matter, it was as if a high wind had come in, rustled, and then blown everyone away. She saw the hall was empty and the front door wide open. While she stood there, Theodore came out of his room.

"What's up?"

"I don't know," said Jane. "Perhaps the horses are out."

She knew and she thought Theodore knew that something else was happening, but the silence in the house had come back and there was no one to answer questions. Then Nurse came from nowhere—from somewhere at the bottom of the stairs—holding up her skirts with a hobbling run. They watched her come up and go in to The Fair Christine. Theodore disappeared, but he was back in a second, buttoning his trousers over his pajama top.

"You stay here," he said, "and look after things. I'm going to find out." In three jumps he was down the stairs.

Staying there was not at all what Jane wanted to do. She wanted to get out of there herself, but Nurse came back with The Fair Christine in her arms and began walking up and down the hall.

"What is it?" said Jane crossly.

"Fire, Miss," said Nurse. "Fire's what it is. Go get your clothes on and wake the children. Ts, ts," she said to the baby.

Jane was dressed in half a minute, but by that time Gander was there—thank heaven—rushing from door to door with orders from Father. They were all to leave the house! "'Tis the rubbish shed, Miss," she said. "'Tis all ablaze."

The rubbish shed was attached to the barn, and the barn

was attached to the house. How could they save it? They had better go as fast as they could. "I'll get Hubert," Jane said.

She had an awful time waking Hubert, and after he was awake, she had an awful time getting him to move. He wanted to stand and think what to take with him and could not decide between a picture of Mother and his cast-iron train with the real boiler. "If I were you," said Jane, "I'd take some clothes."

"That's so," he said, and then couldn't make up his mind about shoes or trousers. Jane harried him and hurried him, not able to keep her feet still. Finally he scraped up the inside of a bureau drawer and put on a cap and was ready. Serafine was on the landing with her bird cage, and Edie had a statue of a horse. Jane went and got Mother's silver-handled riding crop. Gander acted just like a sheep dog. She made no difference in ages, but herded them from the back and would not let them stop on the way to look at what might be happening to the barn. "Get on," she said. "Get on with you now." Jane and Hubert and Serafine solved it by walking backwards, but not for long. The red glow was terrible. They turned back one after the other. "Wow," said Hubert. "It's a goner." Nobody blamed Edie when she began to cry loudly, stumbling through the dark; and when The Fair Christine woke up and began shrieking, too, it seemed the right thing for her to do.

At the McHenrys', where they were supposed to stay while their house burned down, Mrs. McHenry met them at the door and gradually they were put in a room where places were made for them to sleep. There was an enormous bed for Jane, Serafine, and Edie, and Hubert was told he could have fun camping out on the sofa. They all got under the covers meekly.

"Fun!" said Hubert when the door was closed. "What does she take me for!"

Nurse and The Fair Christine were taken off by themselves.

As soon as they were safely alone, they were up again and had pulled aside the curtains and shades. They could see the glow, and somehow from here they could not leave it. They kneeled at the open window without saying anything, except for Edie's shuddering and gulping, and inside themselves they held the flames back, kept them down, put them out with all their might. By the time Edie fell over on the floor and had to be picked up and dumped into the big bed and Jane and Serafine were only keeping themselves up by their teeth on the window sill, they thought maybe they had done it. The glow was fainter, and there were no more sparks shooting up above the barn roof. They were so stiff they had to crawl along the floor to bed.

"I hope Madam's all right," said Jane, remembering they had not seen her at all.

"If anyone had been roasted," said Hubert, crawling up the sofa, "we could smell it from here."

"What I'm thinking of is the poor nags," said Serafine. "They must have been crazy with fright."

"Father and Theodore and Pat could manage them," said Jane confidently just before she went to sleep.

The morning after the rubbish-shed fire, although he had had almost no sleep, Theodore was spending riding his bicycle all over the Milldale pastures. Nothing stopped him. He pushed over hummocks, through grass, over small walls where the front wheel caught and he was bucked off onto the hard pasture ground. He got on again and kept going. He had meant to take Cinder and try all the most dangerous jumps, but at the last minute he couldn't do this. He had, he found, to do the work himself. Any kind of wild work. He could not keep still and see and hear the investigation Father had gone through about how the fire got started. Father had not gone to town this morning, and when the kids had got back from the McHenrys', he had asked everyone to follow him out to the back of the barn. He had let them have a good look at the black remains of the shed, and he had pointed his cane at the charred side of the barn. Then he had asked point-blank, as he stirred the ashes, whether anyone knew how the fire got going. Theodore had heard Serafine clear her throat and saw her touch her lips with the back of her finger before he turned his back and stared at the sky.

"It could have been one of those internal combustions," Serafine said, looking square at Father.

Then, of course, the old man had taken things all wrong.

"Serafine," he had said. "I think it's time you went home. Can you ever tell the truth?"

They had all turned back to the house except Theodore. He had started for the pony stalls, but then had turned distractedly and gone for his bicycle. Already, as he was going up the hill to the Milldale farm, something was seeping over him like drowning. He had not been able to say that he had been smoking behind the barn. And so he, Theodore, had been a kind of liar. He, Theodore, was a sneak himself. He couldn't get over it. He couldn't get away from it, and it was following him no matter what he did.

Theodore started up the biggest hill in the pastures, standing up and pushing the pedals so that his bicycle reared. He worked until his heart was going so hard he thought it must give an awful thump and stop, and then he came crashing down, whacking and leaping from bump to bump. He hoped he would go right straight to hell and be done with it. But no, he got to the bottom alive, and he would have to go home and look at them all and be looked at for the rest of his natural life. Especially by Serafine.

When he got within seeing distance, however, he found the others were not interested in whether they looked at him or not. Already from the top of Grandfather's hill he could see a lot of figures loitering around the front lawn. They reminded him of beagles hunting, but they were slower and seemed to have less sense. He got off his bicycle where Hubert was searching the ground just below the wall. Hubert did not look up for fear of losing his place.

"Bad news," he said. "The black cat's eaten Consuelo."

He and Jane and Edie were searching for the remains.

They wanted to give them decent burial. Serafine had gone somewhere.

Theodore looked himself, half-heartedly. The black cat had gotten into the house, of course, during the investigation and naturally had headed for that darn bird. One awful thing had to happen after the other. He wheeled his bicycle into the circular drive, feeling as if all his blood must have turned black with discouragement. It was just at the horse chestnut tree that he had a clap of thunder inside him. Theodore did not believe in dreams or visions. In fact, Jane would have said he never saw anything. But when he knew he was right, Theodore himself felt that he could see a hundred miles. Right now he saw exactly what the black cat had done with Consuelo. Jumping Jehoshaphat! Cats were so particular, they didn't like to eat off the ground, so they carried things to the boards of the laundry yard and crunched them up there. He leaned his bike on the tree and, avoiding the others, went round the back way. He was right! The old varmint had mangled her prey in a corner under the honeysuckle vine. Theodore stood and looked at it. There was not much left. A bunch of fluff and some tail feathers. But his vision was still telling him what he could do. He picked them up, wiped off a little blood on his trousers, slid them carefully into his pocket, and went into the house. He knew where there was a white candy box in the Rose Parlor with only three pieces of chocolate in it. He emptied these into the pen tray, keeping the frilled paper. He knew where there was a piece of red velvet because he had seen Nurse cutting up Edie's old party dress for a cap for The Fair Christine. He slipped round the house like a shadow, hurrying. In his own room he arranged the remains: first the frilled paper, on top of that the velvet, then Consuelo's tail and fluff. It wasn't quite ready yet. Skinning down the backstairs, he got through the backyard like a fox to Aunt Charlotte's wall and stripped away a bunch of climbing roses. In his room again he scattered these with their golden hearts on the fluff and black feathers. He could not help but think himself that the whole thing looked very well. Now for the try-out!

Theodore tiptoed to Serafine's room with the box held behind him and his eyes on the stairs to see anyone that might be coming. He knocked, but because it was the middle of the day, he went right in. Serafine was lying across the bed. She got up at once and faced him.

"What are you coming in here for?" she said, her face screwed up. "What do you have to interfere for, just when a person doesn't feel well for a moment. Can't you ever leave a person alone?" Theodore was surprised and shocked. She looked like the black cat herself.

"We didn't know you liked the old bird," he said meekly.

"Can't a person like a present from their father," Serafine said, "no matter what it's like?" She glared and pushed her hair back so she could glare better. "I wish you were dead in a pigpen."

"I am almost dead," said Theodore. "Here." He shoved Consuelo's coffin out in front of him. Serafine looked at it, but she did not take it. She turned her back and went and stood at the window, twisting her hands behind her, her shoulders going up and down. Theodore stiffly and cautiously put the box on her bed. Then he backed toward the door.

"I'm sorry," he said. "I'm sorry about absolutely everything. I never was sorrier in my life." He paused to try to find some words on the ceiling. "I puked in the pastures," he said. "Will that satisfy you?"

Serafine had to wait a minute. Then she turned round, using both hands hurriedly to clear her face. She glanced at the box. "There isn't much left," she said, giving one of her little explosive laughs, "is there?" She picked it up and saw how beautifully Consuelo was lying on royal red. "Poooor Theodore," she said sorrowfully and most sincerely.

When Theodore and Serafine came out of the house walking close together, Serafine matching her steps to Ted's, Jane and Hubert, who were lying on the front lawn resting from their labors, turned on their sides and looked after them wonderingly. Hubert got up feeling less tired. He explained to Jane that he had to follow them.

"Spying," said Jane contemptuously, rolling back and closing her eyes.

"Well, I might spy a bit," Hubert said. "Why not? He's been acting so queer lately, he might murder her in cold blood, you know."

He did not have much of a story to tell after his spying, but he was almost queer himself from curiosity. He made Jane the center of a race track and crawled round her asking her to think.

"All they did, absolutely all they did, was crawl like this on their hands and knees under the privet hedge behind the rubbish shed. Now they've both gone bats. I didn't think it was catching. Haven't you got any more brains, Jane? *What* were they doing?"

Jane faced the grass with her head on her arms so that she wouldn't have to see Hubert's crawling. "I don't know," she said, indifferently. "I'm sleepy. I wish you'd keep still. Maybe they just wanted to find out how the fire started."

Hubert decided to take the scab off a mosquito bite for a while. "I never heard of a hedge starting a fire," he said, as he lapped up the nice red blood that came out. "Do you think, do you really think Father will send Serafine home?"

Serafine was not sent home. Nurse told Madam that *she* had taken the sunburst to protect The Fair Christine. "I meant to send the child packing," she said. "But she was too cute for me. How she did ever know that I had it before I could fix that *she* had it, I'll never know."

"I dreamed where it was, Aunt Elsie," said Serafine. "In her work box."

" 'Tis the truth, Madam," said Nurse. "I don't want her vermin bringing diseases into this house, but it is God's truth."

When her family sent for her, however, Serafine had to go, and on the right Monday morning, when the democrat wagon came to the door to take Father to the train, everyone was standing on the steps to help her put in her things.

Theodore had the empty bird cage, Hubert had her suit-case, Jane carried her hat, which she did not want to put on till the last minute, and Edie had a package of sand-wiches. There was half a minute when Serafine was wait-ing beside Ted. Jane saw her put her hand in her pocket, draw it cautiously out, turn the palm in his direction and show him what was there—a long piece of cigarette that had died out after hardly burning at all. Quickly Sera-fine put her hand back and was ready to use it to get in the carriage. After the very last sight of her sitting beside Fa-ther with the bird cage between them had disappeared down the main road, the Cares subsided on the steps silent and empty. Only Theodore moved. He kept pounding one fist into his palm. He gave one good hard pound. "She's a marvelous kid," he said. "A perfectly marvelous kid."

"She's a female," said Jane.

Theodore got up. He put his hands behind his back and raised his chin for air. "I wish to make apologies to the entire sex," he said, bowing deeply to Jane and Edie and the porte-cochère posts, and emphasizing his words with more bows. "I was profoundly mistaken in you all." Then he walked down the piazza and went in, slamming the screen door.